See You
Around, Sam!

Books by Lois Lowry

All About Sam
Attaboy, Sam!
Zooman Sam

Anastasia Krupnik
Anastasia Again!
Anastasia at Your Service
Anastasia Off Her Rocker
Anastasia on Her Own
Anastasia Has the Answers
Anastasia's Chosen Career
Anastasia at This Address
Anastasia, Absolutely

See You Around, Sam!

LOIS LOWRY

Illustrated by Diane deGroat

Houghton Mifflin Harcourt

Boston New York

For information about permission to reproduce selections from this book, write to trade.permissions@hmhco.com or to Permissions, Houghton Mifflin Harcourt Publishing Company, 3 Park Avenue, 19th Floor, New York, New York 10016.

www.hmhco.com

The text of this book is set in Minion Pro.

The Library of Congress has cataloged the hardcover edition as follows:
Lowry, Lois.
See you around, Sam! / Lois Lowry
p. cm.
Summary: Sam Krupnik, mad at his mother because she won't let him wear his new plastic fangs in the house, decides to run away to Alaska.
[1. Runaways — Fiction. 2. Neighborhood — Fiction. 3. Humorous stories.]
I. Title.
PZ7.L9673Se   1996   96–1213
[Fic] — dc20   CIP
AC

ISBN: 978-0-395-81664-6 hardcover
ISBN: 978-0-544-66856-0 paperback

Manufactured in the United States
DOC 10 9 8 7 6 5 4 3 2 1
4500592620

For the Bean

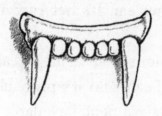

S am?"

Leah's mom, sitting in the driver's seat of the station wagon, turned to look at him. "Here we are at your house. Aren't you getting out? Need help with your seat belt? Can you open the door by yourself?"

Sam shook his head. He had already unbuckled his seat belt with no difficulty. "In a minute," he said. "I need to get something out of my pocket."

"There's your mommy, at the back door," Leah said, pointing. "She has a pencil sticking out of her ear."

Sam wiggled so that he could pull the small object out of his pocket. He didn't look up. "No," he explained. "She always wears a pencil *behind* her ear. It's her carrying place for pencils."

"Sam's mom is an artist," Leah's mom explained to Leah. "So it's probably important for her to have a pencil available all the time. Isn't that right, Sam?"

"Yeah," Sam agreed, but he wasn't really listening. He examined the little object carefully, figuring out which was the front and which was the back. Then he ducked his head so that no one could see, and he inserted it into his mouth. It felt damp, and he realized that it was damp with his friend Adam's spit, and that someone else's spit might be poison. But Sam decided he didn't care.

"Okay," he said, and opened the door of the car.

Mrs. Krupnik had come down to the sidewalk to meet him. Her hair was tied back in a ponytail. She had a yellow pencil tucked behind one ear, as usual, and a coffee cup in one hand.

"Hi, Sam," she said. She smiled at Leah's mom, waved through the window of the car at Leah, and took Sam's hand as he climbed out. "Hot dogs for lunch," she told him cheerfully.

Sam waved to Leah and her mom, but he didn't say goodbye the way he usually did. He was arranging his mouth. His mouth felt kind of uncomfortable, and it might be full of Adam's poison spit, but Sam didn't care. He felt like the coolest guy in the neighborhood. In the town.

He felt like the coolest guy in the whole world.

He held his mom's hand and walked beside her through the yard, up the back porch steps, and across the porch to the kitchen door.

"Sam?" his mom said as she unzipped his jacket in the kitchen. "You're awfully quiet today. Is everything okay?"

Sam nodded. Then, slowly, he smiled at his mother.

She screamed.

It was really cool to make people scream, even your own mother.

"Sam!" his mother said loudly. "What *is* that in your mouth?"

"Fangs," Sam said happily.

He smiled widely. He knew what he looked like, because he had seen Adam smiling just this way at show-and-tell time this morning. Adam had brought the fangs to nursery school.

Sam knew that he looked like Dracula, because he had seen Adam looking like Dracula. Not a fake Halloween costume of Dracula, but the *real* Dracula, with pointy, scary teeth.

Everyone in the nursery school circle had screamed, even the teacher, Mrs. Bennett, when Adam had stood up and smiled. Sam had screamed, too. At first, he had felt very scared. Then, after the scary feeling wore off, he had felt very jealous.

But now *he* had the fangs; they were in *his*

mouth; he had turned into Dracula. And now his mother had screamed.

It was so cool to have fangs.

He was surprised that he could talk when his top teeth were covered with plastic. But he could say "fangs" pretty well, although it sounded a little like "fangsh."

He said it again. "Vampire fangsh."

"Spit," his mother said tensely. She held her hand cupped in front of Sam's mouth.

That was kind of weird, Sam thought. Why would his mother want him to spit into her hand? When the dentist told him to spit, there was a neat little round sink with swirling water for him to spit into.

Anyway, it was hard to spit around the fangs. Sam tried but he didn't manage very well.

"Sam!" his mother said. She jerked her hand away, and wiped it on her denim skirt. She sounded angry now. "I meant spit out the fangs."

Oh. Well, of course he wouldn't be able to eat his hot dog with fangs in his mouth. The hot dog smelled really good. Sam could see it there in the pan on the stove, waiting for him. And the little plastic bottle of bright yellow mustard that squirted from a nozzle — his favorite kind; Sam didn't like brown mustard at all — was waiting by his place at the kitchen table.

So Sam reached into his mouth and carefully took the fangs off of his teeth. He put them into his pocket so that he could find them right after lunch.

Sam was planning to wear the fangs all day. He was already looking forward to greeting his sister, Anastasia, when she came home from school, and his father at the end of the day. He thought maybe his father would be so surprised that he would drop his briefcase and papers would fly all over. That would be exciting.

And he was planning to scare his cat, too. Fangs were so cool.

But his mother was still standing in front of him with her hand out.

"Not in the pocket, Sam," she said. "Give them to me. No more fangs."

Sam closed his hand, inside his pocket, around the fangs. "I traded for them," he explained. "They were Adam's, and he gave them to me, but I have to take him my Etch A Sketch tomorrow."

"Bad trade," his mother said. "Give them to me."

"Why?" he asked. "Why can't I wear fangs?"

"Because it makes you look disgusting," Mrs. Krupnik said.

"That's why I want them," Sam explained. Sometimes mothers don't get it. "I *like* to look disgusting."

"It's just too scary, Sam," his mother said. "Too gross. I saw a terrible movie once, about vampires, and I hated every minute of it, even though Tom Cruise was in it. I've had a thing about fangs ever since. I'm sorry, but I can't let you wear fangs in this house."

Sam frowned. He really wanted his hot dog, but he didn't want to give up his fangs. "How about if I keep them in my pocket?" he suggested.

Mrs. Krupnik thought about it. Finally she sighed. "Promise me you won't take them out of your pocket as long as you're in this house?"

"Even just to look at?"

"Even just to look at. I don't want those fangs to see the light of day. I don't think my heart can stand the sight of those fangs."

"But can I reach into my pocket and touch them?" Sam asked.

"Okay, but don't tell me when you're touching them. I don't want to know."

Sam's hand was in his pocket. "I'm touching them right now," he said.

"Sam! I told you not to tell me!"

"Oh. Okay, now I'm not touching them. Look — here are both my hands. Can I have my hot dog?"

Mrs. Krupnik put their lunch on the table

and poured a glass of milk for Sam and a cup of coffee for herself. Usually she talked to him a lot during lunch. Usually she asked him everything about his morning at nursery school, what songs he had sung and what stories he had heard. But today Mrs. Krupnik didn't say much. "I'm sorry, Sam," she told him as she cleared the empty plates away. She sliced an apple and gave him a couple of pieces. "I just seem to have a thing about fangs. I guess I suffer from fangphobia."

"What's that?"

"Fear of fangs," his mother explained. "Want more apple?"

Sam nodded and she gave him two more slices.

"Do you think maybe you'll get over fangphobia?" Sam asked hopefully. "Maybe by tonight, when Daddy comes home, so I could —"

"Nope. Never."

Sam sighed. He finished his apple slices. "I'm going up to my room," he announced.

"Okay," his mother said, "but remember what you promised, Sam? No fangs. Not in this house."

"I'm going to be very sad up there."

"I'm sorry to hear that. No fangs in this house," she repeated, looking at him.

His mother's face looked very certain, and her voice sounded very certain, so Sam trudged up the stairs to his room with a disappointed feeling. His hand went into his pocket and felt the fangs. His day was ruined.

Somewhere, Sam thought, there would be a nicer place to live. A place where people didn't have fangphobia. Maybe somehow he could find that place.

That was when Sam decided to run away.

2

Quietly, in his bedroom, Sam gathered up the things that he wanted to take with him when he ran away from home.

He found the fireman's badge that he had been given by a real fireman on the day that his nursery school class went to visit a fire station. His mother had planned to sew it to his jacket but she hadn't gotten around to it yet, partly because Sam couldn't choose which jacket.

Very carefully — it took him quite a long time — Sam attached the fireman's badge to the neck of his sweater with a large paper clip that he found in a dish on his sister's desk.

He thought about what else he should take with him. In the bathroom, standing on a chair so that he could reach the medicine cabinet, Sam found a little box of Band-Aids. Sam was very fond of Band-Aids, and especially of these Band-Aids, which were decorated with hearts and stars.

He put several Band-Aids into the pocket of his jeans. But his pocket was already full of fangs, so it didn't feel very comfortable.

He decided maybe it would be better to *wear* the Band-Aids. So, very carefully — it took him quite a long time — he unwrapped three of them, two red and a blue, and stuck them onto himself. Pushing up the leg of his jeans, he stuck one onto his knee, then he stuck another to the back of his left hand. Finally, after a lot of thought, he stuck the third one on his forehead.

Sam climbed on the stool again and examined himself in the mirror.

The fireman's badge was paper-clipped to

the neck of his blue sweater. The Band-Aid, red with white stars, was neatly across his forehead.

He stared at himself for a moment, thoughtfully. It was interesting to see himself with a Band-Aid on his forehead, but what he *really* wanted to see in the mirror . . .

The bathroom door was closed, so maybe it didn't really count as "in the house," and he wouldn't be exactly breaking his promise.

Carefully Sam inserted the fangs into his mouth.

He shuddered a little, looking at himself turned into a werewolf. No wonder his mother had fangphobia. He was really scary to look at.

Thinking guiltily again about his promise to his mother that he would not wear the fangs in the house, Sam replaced them in his pocket. In the mirror, he looked disappointingly normal again, even with a red Band-Aid on his forehead.

Just for the sake of curiosity, Sam tried his mother's eyebrow pencil, which was in a small

basket on the back of the toilet. There were lipsticks in the basket, too, but Sam didn't bother with those. He still remembered playing with the lipsticks when he was much younger, and getting into a lot of trouble.

He darkened his eyebrows a little. He made them bigger than his normal eyebrows, which were quite small. He made his eyebrows into upside-down Vs.

The new dark eyebrows actually looked pretty good with the Band-Aid. They made him look kind of fierce, Sam thought, the way a werewolf or a vampire should look.

He scribbled a little with the eyebrow pencil on his upper lip. He was pretty sure his mother wouldn't mind. It didn't seem to damage the pencil any. And it was *his* upper lip, after all, not anyone else's. The reason she got mad about the lipstick before was because he had scribbled on *her* bedspread.

He gave himself a sort of mustache and scribbled some whiskers onto his chin.

Cool, Sam thought, staring into the mirror.

Back in his room, he found a pair of green mittens. It wasn't very cold out, but Sam didn't know how long he would be gone. Maybe winter would come and he would need mittens.

Then Sam decided that he needed a suitcase.

In the hall closet Sam found what he was looking for. It was his father's gym bag, crimson-colored with the words HARVARD UNIVERSITY on the side.

He took his father's big sneakers out of the bag and put them on the floor of the closet, but he kept the rolled-up towel that he found inside the bag. You could never tell when you might need a towel. Maybe he would wash or something while he was gone.

He added the mittens to the suitcase.

Then, because there was space left in the bag, he added his bear.

Sam had had his bear for a very long time. It had been given to him when he was born, and there were photographs of Sam sleeping in a little crib, with the bear sitting in the corner near his head, at a time when Sam and the bear were both the same size.

Now Sam was, of course, much bigger than the bear. And the bear was a little scruffy, because Sam had chewed its ears when he was a baby beginning to get teeth. But it still slept in his bed, so he decided to take the bear — which had no name — along. The bear had never had any adventures at all, and Sam felt a little sorry for him.

He thought about taking his pajamas, which were hanging on a hook on the inside of his closet door. But he decided not to.

People who ran away probably slept in their clothes, Sam decided. People with fangs wouldn't wear pajamas, especially not pajamas with spaceships on them.

"I'm running away soon," Sam called down the stairs to his mother so she would know. "Because of the fangs," he added.

He listened, but she didn't answer. Mrs. Krupnik had gone into her studio, the large room where she worked at her drawing table doing book illustrations. Probably she hadn't heard him. Sometimes when she was working, his mother didn't notice anything else that was going on.

Well, thought Sam, that was good. He could just sneak away and she wouldn't notice. Probably if she knew he was running away, she would cry and try to stop him.

She would probably scream, Sam thought.

"I'm running *far* away!" he called loudly, and waited for the scream. But there was no answer from the studio.

"Because of the fangs!" he added. But his mother was silent.

Sam trudged back to his room and got his Harvard gym bag suitcase. He thumped the bag down the stairs noisily.

"I'm sorry I'm making all this racket," he called toward the door of the studio, "but I'm taking a big suitcase full of stuff because I'm going to be gone a long time.

"I'm taking mittens," he added, when he got

to the foot of the stairs. "Because when winter comes I'll need them.

"I'll be sleeping in the snow," he called toward the room where his mother was. He could see her back now, in the striped sweater, through the doorway. She was hunched over, working at her drawing table. Her shoes were on the floor and her legs and feet, in black tights, were wrapped around the legs of her special chair.

"Do you hear me?" Sam asked after a minute. "Do you hear me talking?"

His mother turned. She had a pen in her hand and a cheerful expression on her face. "Oh, Sam," she said, with a smile. "Is that you? I heard someone talking, but I didn't think it was you, because the person I heard was talking about running away. So I thought it was a stranger."

"No," Sam said in a serious voice, "it was me."

"I see you are wearing a Band-Aid on your forehead," his mother said with interest.

"Yes. In case I get injured when I'm running away."

"I see. And what is that on your upper lip, Sam?"

"A mustache," Sam explained.

"And attached to your sweater?"

"A fireman's badge."

"In case of . . . ?"

"Well, in case there's a fire," Sam explained.

"I see. You certainly are well prepared, Sam. Do you have your toothbrush?"

Sam shook his head. "People who run away don't brush their teeth," he said. "Anyway," he added, "I'll be wearing fangs."

"Oh, I see," his mother said. "Well, I hope you don't get cavities. I don't know if the dentist is willing to work on fanged people."

"I suppose you're going to cry when I leave," Sam said.

Mrs. Krupnik shook her head. "I don't think so. I'll miss you though, Sam. So will Daddy and Anastasia."

Sam thought for a moment about his father

and sister. Just that morning, at breakfast, all of them had been laughing together in the kitchen.

Anastasia had been talking about Steve Harvey, who lived down the street. Steve Harvey was kind of Anastasia's boyfriend.

"Not anymore," Anastasia had said that morning. "Steve Harvey is *toast*."

"Excuse me?" Mrs. Krupnik had said, looking at the piece of toast in her own hand.

"That means Steve is gonzo," Anastasia explained. "He's not my boyfriend anymore."

"*Kaput*," their father said. He shrugged and laughed. "That means 'toast' in German."

Remembering breakfast, remembering Anastasia and Daddy and how they had all been laughing together, Sam said suddenly to his mother, "I might cry when I run away, even if you don't." He surprised himself saying it, because he hadn't thought of it until just that minute. But suddenly he felt as if he might actually cry.

"Maybe you should pack some Kleenex,"

his mother suggested. "There's some in the downstairs bathroom."

Sam didn't say anything.

"Where are you going, by the way?" his mother asked. "In case we want to write to you."

Sam thought. He hadn't really planned where to go. He thought about fangs and the kinds of places where people with fangs might be welcome.

That made him think about walruses, who had not only giant, scary, sticking-out teeth but also large whiskers. If he had made his pencil mustache larger, Sam thought, it would be almost like walrus whiskers.

"I'm going to be living with walruses," Sam said to his mother, who really seemed to be interested.

"Where might that be?" she asked.

Sam remembered a video he had seen at nursery school. It had shown walruses lying around on ice. They were all asleep, lying in a pile. He thought he remembered that they lived in Alaska. "Alaska," he replied to his mother. "I'll be lying around in a big pile, in Alaska."

"Oh," she replied. "Well, you will certainly need your mittens, then."

"Yes, I will."

"Well, goodbye, Sam. See you around," she said, and waved to him. "I'll miss my number-one super-spectacular son a lot. Especially at dinner. We're having lasagna tonight."

"Bye," Sam said. He picked up his traveling bag and headed for the back door, trying hard not to think about lasagna, and completely forgetting to stop for Kleenex.

I'm toast, he thought, as he let himself out the back door. *Now I'm completely toast.*

3

It was afternoon, and quiet in the Krupniks' neighborhood, with all the school-age children still at school, all the parents still at work, and all the babies taking naps. A few houses down the block, Sam could see Mr. Watson, the mailman, walking along the sidewalk with his heavy mailbag over his shoulder. Sam liked Mr. Watson, who had once run in the Boston Marathon when he was younger; now that he was older, he didn't run much anymore, but he still walked around the Krupniks' neighborhood, carrying his mailbag and delivering the mail.

Lowell Watson had told Sam once that he

thought it was important to keep his hands and his mind both busy. When he was at home, to keep his hands busy, Mr. Watson built things out of pasta. He had told Sam that he had a whole Ferris wheel made from spaghetti and Elmer's glue, and that he was working on a poodle made of curly macaroni. He said that sometime Sam could come and see his pasta creations.

To keep his mind busy, Mr. Watson was trying to learn all the ZIP codes in the United States. It was *very* hard, Mr. Watson said, because there were so many. But he knew all the ZIP codes in Alabama already.

Standing on the porch steps, watching Mr. Watson sort through some mail in his hands, Sam took the fangs from his pocket and arranged them over his own teeth.

There, he thought with satisfaction. He wondered if his mother was looking out the window, feeling sad because her favorite little boy was headed to Alaska to lie around in a pile.

He wondered if she would tap loudly on the window, as she sometimes did, to remind him that he was not allowed to leave the yard.

But behind him the house was silent.

Sam picked up his traveling bag and headed down the steps.

Mr. Watson, spotting him, waved. "Hi, Sam!" the mailman called, walking up to where Sam stood on the sidewalk. "Going on a trip?"

Sam nodded. "To Alaska," he said.

"Wait a minute. Let me think for a minute." Mr. Watson closed his eyes tight and stood silently on the sidewalk. His lips moved a little, and Sam could hear him murmuring, "Nine, nine, six—"

Then he opened his eyes and grinned. "Nine nine six six eight," Mr. Watson said. "That's the ZIP code for Sleetmute, Alaska."

"Sleetmute?"

"Yep. Sleetmute. My goodness, I notice you have fangs, Sam. And a Band-Aid on your forehead."

Sam nodded. "And mittens," he said. "And a mustache."

"Do you have food in your bag? It's a long trip to Alaska."

Sam had forgotten about food. "I'm getting some," he said, deciding that in fact he really would add food to his traveling bag. "I'm getting some from Mrs. Stein." Gertrude Stein, who lived next door, always had homemade cookies available.

Mr. Watson looked toward Mrs. Stein's house. "Well," he said, "I'm headed there myself. I'll go with you and maybe pick up a cookie at the same time."

Mr. Watson adjusted his mailbag so that he had a hand free. He reached down, helped Sam adjust the strap of the Harvard gym bag over his shoulder, and then he took Sam's free hand. Together they walked up the front walk and rang Mrs. Stein's doorbell.

Gertrude Stein answered the door with the telephone receiver in her hand. She smiled and gestured to them to come in.

"I have to go now, I have company arriving at my door," she said into the telephone. "Goodbye."

Mr. Watson stacked Mrs. Stein's mail on the hall table while she hung up the phone. "Sam and I were hoping you had made cookies this morning," he said. "Sam needs cookies because he's heading off on a trip to Alaska and has to fill his bag with supplies. Me, I don't need them at all because I'm ten pounds overweight. But I never pass up your cookies, Gertrude."

Mrs. Stein led them into her kitchen, which, as usual, smelled like chocolate chip cookies. She went to the refrigerator and took out a bottle of milk. "Milk and cookies in the afternoon is a wonderful treat," she said. "Keeps you going for the rest of the day."

She lifted Sam into a kitchen chair and set his traveling bag on the floor beside him.

"I was just talking to your mother on the phone, Sam," she said. "She invited me for dinner tonight. Lasagna."

Sam looked at the plate of cookies and wondered whether he should take his fangs out. Chewing would be terribly hard with fangs.

Lowell Watson arranged his heavy mailbag on the floor in a corner of the kitchen. Then he sat down and reached for a cookie. "That's one of my favorites, lasagna," he said. "Wonder if she has enough for one more guest."

Sam sipped at the glass of milk Mrs. Stein put in front of him. Milk dribbled down his chin and a few drops landed on his fireman's badge.

Gertrude Stein sat down at the other side of the table and passed yellow paper napkins around. Sam noticed, as he always did, how many wrinkles she had on the back of her hands. Mrs. Stein was very old, but she was one of his best friends.

"I always find," Mrs. Stein said casually, "that when I'm wearing fangs, it's a little hard to eat and drink. So I usually take my fangs out temporarily."

"I do, too," Mr. Watson said. "I always take my fangs out at mealtime."

"Even for cookies?" Sam asked.

They both nodded. "Even for cookies," Mrs. Stein said. "The crumbs are a problem with fangs."

"And the chopped nuts," Mr. Watson added. "Am I correct, Gertrude, that you always put chopped walnuts in your chocolate chip cookies?"

"I certainly do. Here, Sam. Have a cookie." Mrs. Stein passed the plate to Sam.

Quickly Sam removed his fangs and put them into his pocket. He bit into a large, warm cookie and felt the slightly melted chocolate in his mouth.

"Mmmmmm," Mr. Watson said. "Delicious as always, Gertrude."

"I'm running away," Sam whispered.

"What was that, Sam?" Gertrude Stein leaned over so that she could hear him better.

"I said I'm running away."

"Oh, yes, I know. Your mother mentioned

it when she called to invite me to dinner. I believe it's why she has extra lasagna available."

"Sam's going to Alaska," Mr. Watson explained. "Sleetmute, Sam? Nine nine six six eight?"

Sam nodded. He decided he would go to Sleetmute.

Mr. Watson finished his milk, rinsed his empty glass in the sink, and picked up his mailbag. "Back to work," he said. "I might see you this evening, Gertrude. When I drop off the Krupniks' mail, I think I'll drop a few hints to Sam's mom about that lasagna."

"She also mentioned a banana cream pie, actually," Mrs. Stein told him.

"More calories," Mr. Watson said. He sighed, closed his eyes, smiled, and licked his lips. Then he took a deep breath and adjusted the strap of the heavy bag. "Thank you once again for the cookies, Gertrude. I wish I could bring you better mail."

Mrs. Stein laughed. "Nothing but bills every time. Well, that's what happens when you get old and don't have any family left."

"And, Sam," Mr. Watson turned to Sam and reached down to shake his hand. "Have a good trip. I'll see you around."

Sam nodded. He and Mrs. Stein both waved to Lowell Watson as the mailman let himself out the front door.

"Maybe you don't have any family left, but you have friends," Sam told Mrs. Stein. "*I'm* your friend."

"That's right, Sam, you are. You're one of my very best friends. I'll miss you when you're in — What was the name of that place?"

"Sleetmute."

"Yes, Sleetmute. It's a very long distance, Sam."

"It's because of fangs," Sam said unhappily. "I'm going to go lie around in a pile."

"I know." Gertrude Stein sounded very sympathetic. "Your mother mentioned that." She rose from her chair. It always took her a little longer than most people, getting out of a chair, because her legs were pretty old and pretty tired and pretty sore.

"Finished?" she asked Sam, reaching for his empty milk glass.

Sam nodded, and she took his glass to the sink.

"More cookies?"

Sam wiped the crumbs from his mouth with his napkin. "Could I maybe have some for my suitcase?" he asked. Then he added, "Please."

Mrs. Stein unzipped his bag and carefully placed a handful of chocolate chip cookies, wrapped in a paper napkin, inside it, next to Sam's bear and on top of the rolled-up towel.

"There you are, Sam. Traveling food." She looked at her watch. "You know," she said, "I always take a nap in the afternoon. So I think I'll lie down on the couch and rest now."

"I used to take a nap," Sam said, "before I ran away."

"My couch has room for two people," Mrs.

Stein told him. "Would you like to lie down with me? I could cover us both up with that nice gray knitted blanket. It's folded right there on the back of the couch." She pointed with her wrinkled hand.

Sam looked through the archway to the living room and saw the thick folded afghan draped over the sofa. "It's green," he told his friend.

Mrs. Stein chuckled. "What ever will I do without you, Sam?" she asked. "Because I have cataracts in both eyes, I can't see colors very well. So I really appreciate your pointing out my mistakes."

Sam peered at her eyes and didn't see anything unusual. But it sounded very scary, having cat-racks.

"And because of my arthritis, I can't walk very well. So I really appreciate having your hand to hold, Sam."

She reached for it, and Sam held her hand while Gertrude Stein made her way to the couch. She lay down with her head on a flowered pillow, and Sam helped her unfold the green blanket.

"Could I visit your flamingos?" Sam asked.

"Of course," Mrs. Stein replied. "I would be very disappointed if you didn't, and so would the flamingos."

Sam went to the downstairs bathroom, which opened off a little hall near the kitchen. He looked at the wallpaper in the bathroom. Sam had seen the wallpaper many times before. Maybe a thousand times. Maybe a million. But still it fascinated him.

Mrs. Stein's bathroom wallpaper was covered with bright pink flamingos. Each one stood on one leg. When he was younger, Sam had thought that the flamingos only had one leg apiece. But now that he was older, and his sister had explained to him about flamingos, he could see that their other legs were all folded up.

Sam always stood on one leg like a flamingo when he visited Mrs. Stein's bathroom. Then he stretched his neck the way the wallpaper flamingos did. (Some of them had their neck bent over so that their head down on their back. Sam couldn't do that part. But he tried to stretch his neck up in the air, and he could feel it being a little flamingo-like.)

He folded his arms like wings and balanced on one leg. It was a good luck kind of thing, doing a flamingo pose.

Sam thought he would need a lot of good luck on his trip to Alaska, so he stood like a flamingo until he lost his balance. Then he went back to the living room, where Gertrude Stein was lying on the couch. She smiled at him.

"Plenty of room right here," Gertrude Stein said, and patted the space next to her. "Join me for a snuggle?"

Sam was tempted. He did feel a little sleepy after the cookies and milk. But his hand had slid into his pocket, and he felt his fangs there, covered in crumbs from a broken cookie. Feeling the fangs made him remember.

"I have to run away," he reminded Gertrude Stein.

She sighed. "My goodness, I had forgotten that, Sam. You're going to that place in Alaska. What was it called again?"

For a moment Sam couldn't remember. Then it came back to him. "Sleetmute," he said.

"Ah, yes. Sleetmute. Well, I hope you enjoy it there, Sam. I wonder if you'd do one more thing for me before you leave."

Sam nodded.

"Could you bring me the telephone from the table? I have to make a phone call, and the cord will reach this far so I won't have to get up on my achy old legs."

Sam lifted the telephone very carefully from the table and brought it to Mrs. Stein.

"And one more thing, Sam, before you go. If you happen to find that you're still in this neighborhood at suppertime —"

"No, I won't be. I'm running away," Sam reminded her.

"Yes, of course, I know that. But just in case you get delayed for any reason, would you stop back here and make certain that I remember to get up? Sometimes I fall asleep in the afternoon and sleep right through dinnertime. But tonight I have an invitation for lasagna and banana cream pie, so I want to be certain not to be late."

"Okay." Sam took his fangs out of his pocket and put them into his mouth. They didn't taste very good, and they were uncomfortable now, covered with crumbs.

"Goodbye," Sam said, with his fangs in.

"Goodbye, Sam," Gertrude Stein replied. As he let himself out the front door, he could hear her dialing the telephone.

"Hello, Katherine?" he heard her say, and realized that Mrs. Stein was talking to his mother.

4

Sam walked slowly back along the side-walk, past his own house. He stood still for a moment, looking at all the familiar things. There was the stubby tower up at the top of the house; his sister's bedroom was in the tower, and she had told him lots of tower stories, like the one about Rapunzel.

Gertrude Stein had told him that when she was a little girl, living in the house where she still lived as an old lady, her friend Edward had lived in the house that was now the Krupniks'. Edward's room had been that very same tower bedroom. He and Gertrude had called messages across the yard to each other from their bedroom windows.

It was so long ago, when Gertrude Stein was a little girl, that probably, Sam thought, the telephone had not yet been invented.

Still looking at the house, Sam could see the windows to his own bedroom. From the sidewalk he recognized the striped curtains. When Sam was much younger, just two years old, he had leaned too hard against one of his bedroom windows, knocked out the screen, and fallen. He couldn't remember that. His head had gotten bashed when he fell and his memory had been bashed right out. But he could remember his stay in the hospital. A nurse had shaved his hair off, and then the doctor had put Frankenstein stitches into his bald head.

Sam was sorry that he hadn't had fangs then. It would have looked really cool to wear fangs when he had Frankenstein stitches and a bald head.

He ran his tongue over the fangs and wished that they felt more comfortable.

Next Sam happened to glance at one of the windows of his mother's studio. He had planned not to look at his mother's windows because he was mad at her still. But his eyes just drifted that way by mistake.

He wondered whether his mother was still in there, still working on the book illustrations, still suffering from fangphobia, still not even caring that her number-one super-spectacular son was headed to Alaska to lie around in a pile.

To his surprise, his mother was looking back at him through the window. He could see that she was talking on the telephone, but she had carried the phone over to the window and just happened to be looking out as he passed. She could see him standing there on the sidewalk.

At first Sam thought that he would pretend not to see her, just to make her feel bad.

But then he decided to smile and wave. So he did that: smiled, showing his fangs, and waved, with the hand not carrying the traveling bag.

His mother smiled and waved back.

That surprised Sam. He had thought that maybe she would start to cry when she saw him, and would rush out and beg him to come home, and maybe she would add more lasagna to the pan so that there would be enough for him at dinner.

But instead she smiled and waved.

Sam trudged on, feeling angry. He tried with his tongue to dislodge a cookie crumb that was stuck under his fangs and was making the top of his mouth hurt.

He decided that he needed a drink of water. The milk at Gertrude Stein's had been good, but now his fangs had a bad taste and he needed water.

He decided to stop for a visit at the Sheehans' house on the other side of his own. There wasn't really any reason to *rush* to Alaska. He could ask Mrs. Sheehan for a drink of water.

He could say goodbye to the Sheehans, who had always been very nice to him, and who had once given him a kitten when they had too many. Also, he could scare Kelly, the Sheehans' baby, with his fangs.

"Come on in, Sam!" Mrs. Sheehan called when he knocked at their back door. It surprised him that she could see through the door and tell who was knocking.

"Nice to see you!" she said cheerfully as he entered, and she folded up her portable telephone and laid it on the counter. "Kelly's daddy's away on a business trip so we're kind of lonely, and it's nice to have company."

She looked more closely at Sam. "Wow, neat fangs!" she said.

The baby was sitting in a playpen in the corner of the Sheehans' big kitchen. Kelly looked up and grinned at Sam.

Sam always wished that the Sheehans' baby had a name like John or Amanda. That way Sam would be able to tell if it was a boy or a girl.

When the baby got a little bigger, maybe it

would wear a dress or a necktie, and then Sam would know. Maybe it would grow longer hair and Mrs. Sheehan would give it a hair ribbon and then Sam would know.

But now it wore overalls and had just a little bit of hair and was named Kelly, and Sam didn't ever know what it was.

If he went off to Alaska, Sam thought — Then he corrected himself in his mind: Not *if*, but *when* he went off to Alaska, he would never find out if Kelly was a boy or a girl.

"Hi, Kelly," Sam said. He leaned over the playpen, feeling a little sad because of the important information about Kelly that he was never going to learn. He grinned a Dracula-style grin so that Kelly would be scared.

But the baby just giggled and looked at Sam with big eyes. He — or she — pointed with a chubby finger toward Sam's mouth.

"Fangs," Sam explained to Kelly. "Maybe when you get bigger, you can have fangs. Your mom wouldn't mind, I bet." He glanced over at Mrs. Sheehan with a questioning look.

"No," Mrs. Sheehan said. "I don't mind fangs."

"*My* mom has fangphobia," Sam told her in a sad voice.

"Yes, she told me," Mrs. Sheehan said. "I have wormphobia myself. I remember that your mom didn't mind when you had a pet worm in your room, Sam. But I'm never going to let Kelly have a pet worm." She looked fondly at the baby. "Got that, Kelly-Belly? No worms?"

Kelly grinned and began to chew on a yellow plastic toy.

Sam set his bag on the floor, unzipped it, reached in, and found his bear wedged beside the rolled-up towel. He took the bear out and handed it to Kelly, who dropped the plastic toy, grabbed the bear, and hugged it.

"Kelly can play with my bear while I visit. But I can't stay long. I have to go to Alaska," Sam told Mrs. Sheehan. "Sleetmute," he added.

"Oh, dear," Mrs. Sheehan said sympathetically. "I was hoping you'd be around next month, Sam, because it will be Kelly's first birthday, and I'm going to have a little party."

"With cake?" Sam asked.

"Yes. And ice cream, of course."

"And presents?" Sam asked.

"Oh, yes, certainly. Lots of presents."

Birthday presents would reveal what Kelly was, Sam realized. "Would the presents be dolls?" he asked. "Or would they be trucks?"

Mrs. Sheehan thought about that. "Probably both," she decided. "Kelly likes both dolls and trucks."

Sam sighed. It didn't matter, really, he realized, since he wouldn't be there for the party, or for Kelly's future, male or female. "I suppose there will be lots of ice cream in Sleetmute," he said.

"Yes, I would expect so."

"I guess I'll live in an igloo, probably," Sam said.

"You'll be eating a lot of fish, I imagine," Mrs. Sheehan said cheerfully.

"*Fish?*" Sam made a face. He didn't like fish

at all. Right now, right at this very moment, there was half of a tuna-fish sandwich hidden behind the radiator in his bedroom.

"And blubber," Mrs. Sheehan added.

"What's that?" Sam asked, wrinkling his nose. He didn't like the sound of it. It was a gross-sounding word: *blubber*.

"Oh, it's a sort of fat," Mrs. Sheehan explained. "From seals, and walruses, I think."

"And you have to *eat* it?" Sam hoped that Kelly's mom was joking, but it didn't really sound like a joke. Her face looked pretty serious.

"Well, if you live in an igloo, I believe your life tends to center around fish, and blubber," Mrs. Sheehan explained.

Sam stood silently for a moment. In the playpen, Kelly chewed happily on a leg of Sam's bear. Sam envied Kelly. It didn't matter if Kelly was a boy or a girl. Kelly would never have to eat blubber.

Kelly would be eating birthday cake in a month. Probably a sweet, crumbly, delicious cake with lots of sticky frosting, Sam thought sadly. At the same time, far, far away in Sleetmute, Alaska, lying around in a pile, Sam Krupnik would be eating a sandwich filled with gray, gluey blubber. Maybe they would let him put some mustard on it, he thought, but somehow the thought didn't cheer him at all.

It didn't seem fair. For a moment Sam had forgotten why, exactly, he was going to Alaska. Then he remembered.

"It's all because of fangs," he whispered to himself mournfully. The word came out sounding like "fangsh" once again. He couldn't even talk right with his mouth full of fangs. Sam pulled them off his teeth and shoved them back into his pocket.

"What was that, Sam?" Mrs. Sheehan asked. "What did you say?"

"It's because of *fangs*," Sam repeated.

Kelly giggled again and banged the bear against the padded floor of the playpen.

5

"Look, Sam, there's your sister," Mrs. Sheehan said. She had been standing near the kitchen window while Sam drank his water. "It must be getting close to four o'clock. I almost always see Anastasia coming home a little before four."

Sam, with his fangs stored in his pocket, finished his drink, put the glass on the table, and peered through the window toward his own house. Sure enough, there was his sister, Anastasia, wearing her L.L. Bean backpack and trotting up the steps of their porch toward the kitchen door.

Usually, when Anastasia got home from school, Sam was in the kitchen. She would come through the door, drop her backpack on the table, and say, "Hey, Sam." It was what she always said. Sam liked the sound of it: "Hey, Sam." It made him feel kind of grown up.

She would go to the refrigerator and find something to eat. Anastasia liked leftover stuff. Thinking about it, Sam remembered that they had had chicken for dinner the night before.

Right now, right at this very moment (because his sister had gone in now through the kitchen door), he imagined Anastasia would be taking leftover chicken from the refrigerator. If Sam were there in the Krupniks' kitchen, instead of running away to Alaska, she would be sharing leftover chicken with him.

On an ordinary day, not a running-away day, Sam would sit there at the kitchen table with Anastasia, sharing their snack. His mom would ask how school was that day, and Anastasia would tell them funny stories, like once she told how a girl named Marlene got the flu and threw up in her locker.

And once Anastasia had told him about a classmate, a seventh grade boy named Jacob Berman who was a teacher's pet. Sam didn't know what "teacher's pet" meant. At first he thought Anastasia was describing a boy who slept on the floor beside the teacher's bed and maybe went for walks on a leash now and then.

But Anastasia had explained that "teacher's pet" didn't mean the same as family pets, like her goldfish, or Sam's kitten. "Teacher's pet" meant like Eddie Haskell on *Leave It to Beaver*, that Jacob Berman talked in a fake way to the teacher so the teacher liked him but nobody else did.

Anyway, Anastasia said, Jacob Berman had memorized a long, long poem about a guy named Ancientmariner. Ancientmariner was on a boat, and he hung a dead bird on a string around his neck, and everybody on the boat died. It sounded really interesting to Sam.

But when Jacob Berman stood up in front of Anastasia's English class and recited it for extra credit, it was so long and so boring that half the class — and the teacher, too — all fell asleep.

Anastasia said that there was a part in the poem where Ancientmariner said, "And they all dead did lie; and a thousand thousand slimy things lived on . . ." When Jacob Berman said that part, Anastasia described, he looked at the class, and half of them had their heads on their desks, and even the teacher's mouth was hanging open and he was snoring.

Sam didn't see how a poem about dead guys and a thousand thousand slimy things and a guy who wore a dead bird could possibly be boring. But Anastasia had said, "Take my word for it, Sam, it *was*."

Sam stood there looking out of Mrs. Sheehan's kitchen window, toward his own family's kitchen window, and thought about Anastasia inside that kitchen, eating leftover chicken and telling interesting stories to his mother, and the two of them laughing.

He thought that Anastasia would probably be asking, right about now, "Where's Sam?"

"Here I am!" Sam called softly through the closed window of the Sheehans' kitchen. "I'm over here!" His breath made a steamy little cloud on the cool glass pane and he wiped it with his hand.

For a moment he thought that Anastasia might magically hear him, come to the Krupniks' window, and wave across the yard. But she didn't.

"Can I give you any other supplies for your trip, Sam?" Mrs. Sheehan asked. She had just folded an old pink and blue plaid baby blanket and put it into his bag, so that he would be warm during blizzards in Sleetmute. "Do you have everything you need?"

Sam thought for a moment, remembering what was in his traveling bag. Blanket, mittens, cookies, towel. His bear was still in Kelly's playpen, but he would get it back before he headed out.

"I wish I had a portable phone," he said, looking longingly at the little folded-up phone on Mrs. Sheehan's counter. Back at his own house there were only boring phones attached to the wall.

"Yes," Mrs. Sheehan agreed, "that would be nice. You could call your family often if you had a portable phone in your bag. I'm afraid I don't have an extra one to give you, though."

"Anyway, I wouldn't call my mom, because I don't like her anymore," Sam said.

"Yes, that's right. I'd forgotten."

"Because of fangs," Sam said.

"Yes, because of fangs. Of course."

He and Mrs. Sheehan sat silently for a moment. In the playpen, Kelly had set the bear aside and was chewing on a board book about farm animals. There were little teeth marks on the cow and calf page.

"You might want to call your dad and sister,

though, if you had a phone," Mrs. Sheehan said.

"Yes. I might."

"In fact," Mrs. Sheehan suggested, "maybe you'd like to call your sister right now, before you head off to Alaska."

"Sleetmute," Sam said.

"Yes, before you go to Sleetmute. You didn't have a chance to say goodbye to Anastasia. Would you like to use our telephone?"

Sam nodded. It seemed like a good idea.

Mrs. Sheehan unfolded the telephone and dialed for him. Sam heard her talk briefly to his mother.

"Katherine," he heard her say, "Sam would like to talk to Anastasia. He wants to say goodbye before he leaves for Alaska."

She waited a moment, then handed the telephone to Sam. "Here's your sister, Sam," she said.

"Hello?" Sam said.

"Hey, Sam!" He heard Anastasia's voice. Always when his sister said "Hey, Sam!" it made him feel grown up and special. But for some reason, this time it made him feel sad. It made him feel like crying.

Anastasia didn't notice. "I wish you were here, Sam," she said. "I had a chicken leg all saved for you, and then Mom told me you weren't even home. She said you had run away."

"Because of fangs," Sam whispered into the telephone.

"Yeah, that's what she said. You know what, Sam? Once, when I was younger, I ran away."

"Because of fangs?"

"Nope. It was because of *you*."

"*Me?*"

Anastasia started to laugh. "Wait'll I tell you! But it's too long a story for the phone. How about if I come over to the Sheehans' house? You're not leaving right away, are you? I know you have a long trip and you might want to get started."

Sam sighed. Holding the telephone to his ear, he looked through the Sheehans' window to the street, and to the sidewalk that led to the corner. He didn't even know which direction Alaska was.

He was afraid it would be dinnertime soon, and then dark, and bedtime, and he would be all alone on that sidewalk not knowing the way to Sleetmute.

He didn't like thinking about any of that.

"Could you bring the chicken leg?" he asked his sister. "When I'm not wearing my fangs, I can eat a chicken leg."

"Sure."

"Okay," Sam said. "Come on over."

Mrs. Sheehan took Kelly upstairs for a bath, and left Sam alone with Anastasia in the kitchen. They sat together in the little place called the breakfast nook. Sam liked the breakfast nook. It was a sort of a booth, like at McDonald's, and there were red cushions on the seats. A wooden holder shaped like a rooster held paper napkins. Anastasia gave Sam a napkin along with his chicken leg.

Sam felt better now that he was eating the leftover chicken leg, which tasted just as good as it had last night at dinner. He felt better now that Anastasia was here. He felt stronger. He wondered if maybe she would be willing to go to Alaska with him.

"Tell me about when you ran away because of me," he said to his sister.

"Well," Anastasia said, "I was older than you. I was ten. You weren't even born yet."

"How could you run away because of me then, if I wasn't even born?" Sam asked with interest. He licked his fingers. They were greasy from chicken and tasted good.

"Mom and Dad had just told me that they were expecting a baby."

"Me!" Sam announced happily.

"Yes. Of course they didn't know it was you. It was just a baby. After you were born, you were *you*, but before you were born, we didn't know you were going to be you."

Sam didn't quite understand all that, but he nodded his head and pretended that he did.

He wanted to hear the part about running away.

"Anyway," Anastasia went on, "I was the only child up till then. And I didn't like the idea of sharing Mom and Dad."

"You're good at sharing," Sam pointed out. It was true. Anastasia was much better than he at sharing.

"*Now* I am. But it took me a while. And when they told me there was going to be a new baby, I got mad. I wanted them all to myself."

Sam nodded. He could understand that feeling.

"So I told them I was running away, and I packed a bag. You know a funny thing, Sam?"

"What?"

Anastasia was looking at the traveling bag on the kitchen floor near the breakfast nook. "Well, I see that you've borrowed Dad's gym bag. The funny thing is that when I ran away, I took a bag of Dad's too. It wasn't the same one, though. I took his old Navy bag. You know the one with his name — KRUPNIK M— stenciled on the side?"

Sam did remember the bag his sister was talking about. It was much bigger than the one he had packed, and it had a drawstring at the top. "I can't take that one," he said, "because I'm KRUPNIK S, not KRUPNIK M."

"Well, that didn't bother me. I took that bag and I put a whole lot of stuff in it. Food, and clean socks, and — let's see — my watercolors, and some souvenirs. I remember that I felt very, very sad that I couldn't pack my goldfish."

"Yeah. I feel very sad about my cat," Sam said gloomily.

"And I told Mom and Dad that if they were serious about having another baby, I would be moving out."

"And did you? Did you move out? How long were you gone? How far did you go? Was it cold where you went?"

Anastasia adjusted her glasses. She scrunched up her face the way she always did when she was thinking. "No, I didn't ever leave. I'm trying to remember why I didn't."

"Probably they locked you in the house," Sam said. "Maybe they tied you up." Actually, he was wondering why his mom hadn't locked him in the house, or tied him up.

"No, they didn't. They stayed very cheerful, I remember. They helped me pack."

Rats, thought Sam. Just like Mom this very afternoon.

Anastasia scrunched her face again. "I wish I could remember why I stayed," she said.

"I know!" Sam announced. "I bet they said okay, they changed their minds, and they wouldn't have another baby after all. Just like Mom will probably change her mind and say, 'Guess what, Sam, I've been doing some thinking about those fangs, and —'" He stopped in the middle of his sentence and looked at his sister.

"No, they didn't change their minds, did they?" he said.

She shook her head, smiling at him. "You

were already on your way. Here you are. That's proof."

"You changed *your* mind, then," Sam said.

Anastasia nodded her head yes. "I remember," she said. "They told me that if I changed my mind, if I decided to stay, if I didn't run away after all, I could name the baby."

"Me," Sam said with satisfaction.

"Yes, you. I stayed, I unpacked my bag, and when you were born, I gave you your name."

"Thank you," Sam said politely.

"You're welcome. You know what, Sam?"

"What?"

Anastasia sighed. "It really makes me very sad that my only brother, the person I named, is going off to Alaska."

It made Sam very sad, too. But he didn't want to admit it.

"Maybe you'd like to go with me," he suggested.

"No," Anastasia replied. "I wouldn't. We're having lasagna for dinner tonight.

"You know what else, Sam?"

"What?"

"It's considered very grown-up to change your mind after you've thought something over. Mom and Dad thought it was very mature of me to change my mind that time, about running away."

Sam sighed. He didn't know what to say. Finally he reached into his pocket and took out the cookie-crumb-covered fangs. Carefully he inserted them into his mouth, wedging them painfully over his front teeth. Now they tasted like a combination of old plastic, used spit, stale milk, and chicken grease.

One side of his upper lip was caught on the edge of a fang. He adjusted it with his hand. He stared at Anastasia mournfully and she stared back.

"That's really cool, Sam," she said at last. "Maybe I should have named you Dracula."

6

Anastasia looked at her watch. "It's getting late, Sam. I have homework, and I have to do an errand for Mom first."

Sam frowned. Usually he was Mrs. Krupnik's errand-runner. He hadn't even left for Alaska yet, and already other people were getting his jobs.

"What sort of errand?" he asked his sister. The words came out all weird, so he removed his fangs. He stuck them back into his pocket and tried talking again. "What errand?"

"I told Mom I'd go across the street and check on Mr. Fosburgh. She called to invite him over for dinner tonight — she's making lasagna —"

"I know." Sam scowled. He didn't like being reminded of the lasagna, especially now that he was looking ahead to a lifetime of blubber.

"But he didn't answer the phone," Anastasia explained. "Probably he was just taking a nap, but I told Mom I'd check."

"Mrs. Stein is taking a nap," Sam said, suddenly remembering something. "I told her I'd wake her up before I leave for Alaska."

"Okay. Want to come with me first to Mr. Fosburgh's?"

Sam agreed, and he began to pack his bag again. He leaned over the rim of Kelly's playpen, steadying himself with one hand so that he wouldn't fall in. He picked up his bear, folded its legs, and curled it into the bag on top of the rolled-up towel and next to the knitted baby blanket that Mrs. Sheehan had given him. He smoothed the green mittens and replaced them next to the bear. He checked Gertrude Stein's cookies, mostly broken now, and noticed that Mrs. Sheehan had quietly tucked some additional food, two oranges and a small jar of peanut butter, into his bag.

That would probably last him until he got to Sleetmute and learned to eat blubber.

"Maybe they make peanut butter and blubber sandwiches in Sleetmute," Sam suggested hopefully to Anastasia.

"Maybe. Blubbernutters, those would be called," she said.

"Do you think blubbernutters would taste better than tuna fish?" Sam asked.

Anastasia thought about that. "No, actually, I'm afraid they wouldn't, Sam. But I suppose you could learn to like them, especially if there wasn't much else to eat."

Sam thought about Alaska, and what else they might have there, in addition to blubber. He remembered, from the same film that had shown walruses lying around in a pile, that there were many bears in Alaska. "I could eat bear, maybe," he suggested. "Bear meat sandwiches. Bearwiches."

Anastasia nodded and laughed. "Of course, you'd have to watch out that the bears didn't make Samwiches first."

Sam could tell that his sister was joking, that she thought it was funny, that it didn't scare her at all. But Sam didn't laugh. He didn't like the thought of Samwiches and he wished that she hadn't said it.

Sam took his fangs out of his pocket one more time and examined them, trying to figure out why they had become so uncomfortable. He picked off several cookie crumbs and a piece of walnut. Then, once more, painfully, he replaced the fangs over his teeth. He zipped his jacket.

"Bye, Mrs. Sheehan! We have to go!" Anastasia called up the stairs.

"Bye, Anastasia!" Mrs. Sheehan called back. They could hear Kelly laughing and splashing in the tub. "Thanks for coming by! You too, Sam. See you around! If you change your mind about running away, I'll send you an invitation to Kelly's birthday party!"

"Okay," Sam said glumly, heading for the door. His traveling bag felt bulky and awkward. It had seemed heavy before, but now, with the peanut butter jar and the oranges, it *really* was heavy. His fangs felt terrible. Sam felt weak, small, lonely, scared of bears, and unhappy about blubber, and he didn't know the way to Alaska.

He took his sister's hand and they crossed the street to Mr. Fosburgh's house.

Sam liked all of the people in their neighborhood. But Mr. Fosburgh was one of his very favorites, because Mr. Fosburgh had a motorized wheelchair and he sometimes let Sam sit on his lap, ride in the chair, and operate the switches.

"Blast off!" Sam would say, sitting on Mr. Fosburgh's knees. Then he would push the forward switch so that they would whirr slowly through the first floor of Mr. Fosburgh's house.

Mr. Fosburgh had shown him how to turn right, or left, and how to reverse, and to stop.

It was a whole lot more fun than the

mechanical horse in front of the supermarket. Sam always thought the horse would be fun, and he always begged and begged his mom until finally she would say "Oh, all right," and she would find some money to put into the slot. Then Sam would sit on the big plastic horse, hoping that this time it would really gallop and whinny; but it never did anything but jiggle silently up and down, which was boring.

You didn't even have to put quarters into Mr. Fosburgh's wheelchair. Mr. Fosburgh's wheelchair was *free*.

"Coming!" Sam and his sister could hear Mr. Fosburgh's voice through the door after they rang the doorbell.

They could hear his chair whirr into the hall.

"Well, it's the Krupniks!" Mr. Fosburgh said with a smile when he opened the door. Then he looked again. "At least it's Anastasia. But who is that? It's the size of Sam, and it's wearing Sam's jacket, but it has a strange unSamlike look." He peered at Sam's face.

"It's me, Sam Krupnik, with a mustache and big eyebrows," Sam explained.

"I see that. But what are those other things?"

"Fangs," Sam said. He took them out of his mouth and held them up so that Mr. Fosburgh could get a closer look.

"Oh, of course, fangs." Mr. Fosburgh smiled, but he looked a little puzzled. "I had fangs when I was young, but the orthodontist got rid of them for me." He smiled broadly so that Sam could see his teeth, which were stained beige from cigarettes but nice and straight, with no fangs.

Sam was astonished. "An octopus took your fangs?" he asked.

"Orthodontist," Anastasia said. "That's the kind of dentist who puts braces on your teeth and straightens them. Go on in, Sam, so we can close the door. It's cold out here." She nudged Sam inside.

"Mom called, but you didn't answer the phone," Anastasia explained to Mr. Fosburgh. "She wanted to invite you over for lasagna tonight."

"Lasagna!" Mr. Fosburgh's face lit up. At the same time, the end of his cigarette lit up as he inhaled on it. Poor Mr. Fosburgh couldn't manage to stop smoking. He had tried a million times. "My favorite! I'd love to. Thanks, Anastasia.

"My phone's out of order," he explained. "And I couldn't figure out how to call the telephone company and tell them, because of course I need a phone to call them, but mine's out of order. Now, there's a problem, right, Sam?"

"Right," Sam agreed, nodding his head. He had just noticed something. When Mr. Fosburgh talked with a cigarette in his mouth, he had to squint and scrunch his face. It was a little like trying to talk with fangs. Sam put his fangs, which were still in his hand, back into his pocket.

"But I could call from your house, if I come over for dinner," Mr. Fosburgh said. "Right now, though, it looks as if Sam needs a ride. How about it, Sam? Let me just put out this nasty cigarette."

Mr. Fosburgh mashed his cigarette into one of the nearby ashtrays and lifted Sam up onto his knees. They whirred down the hall with Sam's hand on the controls. Anastasia followed, carrying Sam's traveling bag.

Mr. Fosburgh's arm was around Sam, and his fingers felt the edge of the medallion attached to Sam's sweater. "What's this?" he asked.

"My fireman's badge."

"Oh, I'm so glad you're wearing your fireman's badge, Sam," Mr. Fosburgh said. "It makes me feel very secure, having fire department representatives living in the neighborhood. You know about my problem, of course." Mr. Fosburgh's voice was a little embarrassed.

Sam nodded. Poor Mr. Fosburgh just couldn't stop smoking. Sometimes he dropped a lighted cigarette and wasn't able to retrieve it because he had difficulty walking. So sometimes he set his house on fire. The hook-and-ladder truck had had to save Mr. Fosburgh's house — and Mr. Fosburgh, too — three times in the past year.

"I rely on people like you, Sam," Mr. Fosburgh said. "Whatever would I do without people like you?"

In the past, when Mr. Fosburgh said that, it always made Sam feel proud and important. Now, though, he felt terrible. He didn't know what to say. He sat very still on Mr. Fosburgh's lap. He looked at the floor. There was a small dark burn mark on the floor from a dropped cigarette.

"I'm sorry to tell you that Sam is moving to Alaska," Anastasia said in a sad voice.

Mr. Fosburgh craned his neck around in order to look at Sam, who was sitting silently on his lap, looking down at the floor.

"Sam? Is that true?" Mr. Fosburgh asked in astonishment.

Sam nodded. "Because of fangs," he whispered. His voice came out funny.

"My mom hates his fangs," Anastasia explained.

"Fangphobia," Sam whispered.

Mr. Fosburgh nodded. "I see," he said. "It's like my cigarettes."

Sam wiggled around to look at him. "Why is it like your cigarettes?" he asked.

"Everybody hates my cigarettes. Your mom does. So does your dad."

"So do I," Anastasia pointed out.

Mr. Fosburgh nodded. "So when I go to your house, Sam — like tonight, when I go there for a great lasagna dinner — I leave my cigarettes at home. I wouldn't dream of putting a cigarette into my mouth in the presence of a wonderful woman like your mother."

Sam ran his fingers over his fangs. He thought about it. It made sense to him, what Mr. Fosburgh had said. "But it's my house, too. I can't leave my fangs at home because I *am* at home there."

"That's a problem," Mr. Fosburgh agreed.

"So I'm running away."

"To Alaska, you said?"

Sam nodded. "Sleetmute."

"Sleetmute? Let's check it out. Full speed ahead, Sam. Whirr me to the globe."

Sam pushed the handle and directed the wheelchair down the hall, then to the right, into the den where the huge globe stood on its three-legged stand near the window. He whirred himself and Mr. Fosburgh up close to the globe, and Anastasia joined them.

Mr. Fosburgh leaned forward and clicked a switch that lighted the globe from inside. The whole world became beautiful colors; the oceans were pale blue, dotted with tiny pink islands, and Sam could see the familiar shape of the United States, which he had on a placemat at home. Sam knew how to find his own state, Massachusetts, on his placemat, and he could see that it was in the same place on Mr. Fosburgh's globe.

Mr. Fosburgh turned the globe carefully.

"I'm sorry to tell you that there's a cigarette burn on western Canada. I leaned too close to the globe when I was examining Lake Athabasca once." He slowed the globe. "Here, Sam. Here's Alaska. See?"

Sam looked where Mr. Fosburgh's finger was pointing. Alaska was very far away from Massachusetts. Very, very, *very* far away.

Mr. Fosburgh had leaned close to the globe, and to Alaska, and was squinching his eyes. "No sign of Sleetmute," he announced. "Anastasia, hand me the atlas, would you?"

Anastasia got the huge book from its shelf, and Sam climbed down from Mr. Fosburgh's lap so that they could open the atlas across his knees.

Mr. Fosburgh propelled his finger across Alaska and then stopped. "Bingo! Here it is. Sleetmute."

Sam looked. So did Anastasia. Nobody said anything for a moment.

Then Anastasia said, "It's sort of in the middle of nowhere."

"Well," Mr. Fosburgh suggested, "it's probably very beautiful. No doubt great scenery, Sam."

Sam nodded.

"A little cold in winter, I expect. But you probably have lots of warm clothing in your bag."

Sam nodded again. "I have mittens," he told Mr. Fosburgh, "and a blanket. I have my bear, too.

"And," he added, "I'll be lying around in a pile."

"I remember your bear," Mr. Fosburgh said. "He's been here to visit. Well, Sam, your bear will be in good company in Sleetmute. I'm fairly certain there will be a lot of live b —"

"Don't talk about that," Sam said suddenly. "Please," he added, to be polite.

Mr. Fosburgh closed the atlas. "I understand," he said sympathetically. "We won't discuss wildlife, then."

Wildlife. It had been scary enough, Sam thought, when people had mentioned bears.

But now they had said that other word: *wild-life*. It made him shiver inside. It made him think of all kinds of beasts, with claws and growls and roars — and fangs.

Quietly he reached into his pocket and touched the wet, crumb-covered chunk of white plastic. He stood there in Mr. Fosburgh's living room, staring at the brightly lit globe, where Massachusetts looked small and cozy, and Alaska looked very large and very cold and very far away.

7

"My dad will come over to get you when he gets home from work," Anastasia told Mr. Fosburgh. They walked back toward the front door while Mr. Fosburgh glided beside them in his chair, the atlas balanced on his lap.

"Fine. I'll change my shirt and smoke a last cigarette or two. Then I'll brush my teeth and gargle some mouthwash so that your mother won't have to smell the tobacco."

"Have you tried hypnotism, Mr. Fosburgh?" Anastasia asked. "My friend Daphne's mom went to a hypnotist and quit smoking that way."

"No, but I'm going to try that next, I think."
Mr. Fosburgh sighed. Then he looked at the
atlas on his knees. "You know what, Sam?"
he said. "You're going to need a good map for
your trip. Here. Unzip your bag and I'll put
this in, as a farewell gift."

Sam pulled open the zipper of his traveling
bag. Mr. Fosburgh leaned over from his chair
and wedged the atlas on top of the curled up
bear.

"Thank you," Sam said politely, although
he didn't actually feel very grateful. He knew
Mr. Fosburgh was correct, that he would need
a map. But Sam didn't have any idea how to
read a map. And the atlas made his traveling
bag so heavy that now he had to use two hands
to carry it, and it thunked against his knees.

Thinking about his knees, Sam remembered something else that he would probably
need in Alaska.

"I forgot to bring Band-Aids," he said. "I
have the ones that I stuck on myself. But what

if I need new ones in Alaska?" (He was *really* thinking *Because of bear bites*, but he didn't say it.)

"Well, we have to go over and wake Mrs. Stein up from her nap. Maybe she has a few extra Band-Aids that you can have," Anastasia suggested.

"Mom does. Mom has these Band-Aids with stars and hearts on them, like this one." Sam said hopefully. He pushed his hair back so that his sister could see the Band-Aid across his forehead.

"I thought you were mad at Mom," Anastasia reminded him.

"I am. I don't like her anymore. But I still like her Band-Aids."

Anastasia sighed and opened the door to Mr. Fosburgh's front porch. "Got everything, Sam? Where are your fangs?"

Sam patted his pocket.

"Zip your jacket. It's getting chilly."

Sam zipped his jacket. If it was chilly now,

in October, in Massachusetts, he wondered what it would be like in winter, in Sleetmute. He began to worry about his ears.

At nursery school there was a picture book about Eskimo children. They all wore parkas with fur hoods.

"I think I need a fur hat," Sam said.

"Well," Anastasia said impatiently, "you should have thought of that before you decided to go to Alaska. You should have made a shopping list."

"I could ask for a fur hat for Christmas," Sam suggested.

"Fine. You do that. We'll mail you a fur hat to Alaska. Or Santa Claus can just drop one down the chimney of your igloo."

Sam remembered, suddenly, that Santa Claus lived up near Alaska somewhere. Santa Claus had a hat with fur, and he had mittens and boots.

Looking at himself, at his own light jacket, blue jeans, and sneakers, and remembering not only Santa Claus but also the picture book that showed Eskimo children bundled up with their faces barely showing, Sam began to feel that maybe he was not well prepared for winter in Sleetmute.

He wished that someone else would notice. But Mr. Fosburgh was lighting a cigarette and Anastasia was looking at her watch.

"Come on," his sister said. "It's time to go wake up Mrs. Stein so she can get ready to come over for dinner. Look, Sam, it's starting to get dark out already."

Standing on Mr. Fosburgh's porch, Sam looked around the neighborhood and could see that the sun was beginning to set. The trees along the sidewalk were making long shadows that seemed to reach across the street. Lights were beginning to appear in people's windows.

After they woke up Mrs. Stein, he thought, and Anastasia went back home, he would be all alone. By then it would probably be seriously dark and very scary. Sam had never been outdoors alone after dark.

"I don't like the dark a whole lot," he said

timidly. "I'm not *scared* of it," he added. "I just don't like it."

Mr. Fosburgh, about to close the door behind them, said, "Gee, Sam, you probably ought to start learning to like the dark. In Alaska, in the winter, it's dark all day long.

"See you later, Anastasia," he said. "And, Sam, I guess I won't see you later. So this is goodbye. I will truly miss you. I hope you'll send me postcards from Alaska. I especially would like to hear about the wildlife around Sleetmute."

"Is it really dark *all day long?*" Sam asked suddenly.

"Only in winter," Mr. Fosburgh said. "Of course, winter's on its way right now."

"I don't have a flashlight!" Sam wailed.

"One minute," Mr. Fosburgh said. He whirred his wheelchair in reverse to the hall table, reached into a drawer, and whirred back. "Here you are. It's a small one. I think it'll fit into your pocket."

Sam took the miniature flashlight from

him. He forgot to say thank you. "My pocket is full of fangs," he said. "There's no room for even a little flashlight."

"I thought you intended to *wear* your fangs, Sam," Anastasia pointed out. "Wasn't that the whole point of running away? So that you could wear fangs?"

So once again Sam took the fangs from his pocket and inserted them into his mouth. He made a face. They felt terrible, tasted terrible, smelled terrible. He tried to arrange his lips more comfortably, but it was impossible.

He tested the little flashlight. When he pressed its switch and pointed it at Mr. Fosburgh's doormat, a feeble beam of light appeared.

"It's not a very powerful light, Sam, and the batteries are a little weak," Mr. Fosburgh said from the doorway. "You wouldn't be able to see a large herd of animals with it. But I believe it'll throw enough light to show one creature at a time."

"Creature?" Sam wiggled the little light at

the doormat. Somehow the word "creature" was just as terrifying as the word "wildlife." He thought that he could see a creature on the doormat: just a small creature, maybe an ant.

"Like an ant?" he asked Mr. Fosburgh, wiggling the light again.

"I was thinking more along the order of a bear," Mr. Fosburgh said. "I believe you could illuminate one bear at a time with that flashlight. At least you could if it was a small bear. Not a grizzly."

"Don't say grizzly," Sam whispered.

He clicked the flashlight off. Now, in the dusk, he couldn't see the ant creature at all. It could be walking right toward his sneakers and he wouldn't see it.

If he were in Alaska, and it was dark all the time, and the creature was a bear, and his flashlight batteries died, the bear could be walking toward his sneakers and he wouldn't see it at all.

There could be all sorts of wildlife coming

toward him, and he wouldn't know. He would just be lying there in a pile, in the dark, hatless and cold and chewing on blubber.

"Sam, good luck. I'll see you around," Mr. Fosburgh said cheerfully. "Anastasia, I'll see you later for lasagna." He closed the front door and Sam could hear his chair whirr away down the hall.

See you around, Mr. Fosburgh had said. Mrs. Sheehan had said the same thing. So, he remembered, had Mr. Watson. Sam tried to figure out what it meant, exactly. See you around what? It sounded as if they were all in a circle, like people playing Farmer in the Dell. People in a circle could see each other around.

But Sam, according to the globe in Mr. Fosburgh's study, was not in a circle. Not anymore, at least. Sam was heading in a long, straight line from Massachusetts to Alaska.

Nobody, he realized, was going to see Sam Krupnik around.

Anastasia started down the steps of the porch. Behind her, Sam pushed the little flashlight into his pocket. He adjusted his foul-tasting fangs and wiped his eyes, which seemed to be starting to cry a little bit. He picked up the heavy traveling bag with both hands and followed his sister down the steps, maneuvering the bulky bag and stumbling along after it.

"Sam, I certainly am pleased to see you!" Gertrude Stein smiled as she opened the front door. "I was afraid maybe you wouldn't stop back here again, that you'd be off to Alaska without a final goodbye kiss from me."

"I promised to wake you up, remember?" Sam asked. Hearing the clumsy way his words came out, he sighed and removed his fangs again. He shoved them into his pocket with the flashlight.

"Of course I remember. And you've brought your sister, too. Hello there, Anastasia."

She ushered them inside. The lights were on, now that it was beginning to be twilight.

Sam looked around, thinking that it was the last time he would be here. He tried to memorize Mrs. Stein's house so that when he was in Sleetmute, living in an igloo, lying in a pile, he would never forget the warm and cozy places of his past.

"You have nice old-fashioned stuff," Sam said.

Mrs. Stein nodded. "Yes, I do, don't I? This is the house where I was born and I've lived here almost eighty years. This was my mother and father's furniture. They don't make furniture like this anymore.

"See this table?" Mrs. Stein pointed to the hall table where the telephone was. "This is a real antique. Know how you can tell? Look at the feet."

Sam looked with interest at the table's feet, and saw that they were carved from wood to look like real animal feet, with toes and toenails, and that they were grasping a wooden ball, as if they were about to go bowling.

His sister was looking, too. "Those are really weird," Anastasia said.

"Those are called ball-and-claw feet," Gertrude Stein explained.

"*Claw?*" Sam repeated nervously. People seemed to be saying a lot of scary words lately, now that he was about to leave for Alaska.

Mrs. Stein nodded. "They look almost like eagle talons, don't they?"

Talons. She was doing it again: saying a scary word as if it were just ordinary. Sam shuddered, thinking of talons and claws.

"Sam might see eagles in Alaska," Anastasia said. "There are a whole lot of eagles there. I saw it on a *National Geographic* special not too long ago."

"That's right!" Mrs. Stein agreed. "Sam, be sure to write and tell us when you see eagles. Wouldn't it be wonderful if you saw one actually swoop down and catch something in its talons?

"Look!" Mrs. Stein began to laugh. She

held up her own hand, gnarled with arthritis. "I have eagle claws myself!"

"Gotcha!" She reached over and grasped Sam gently by his ear.

Sam shuddered. He wondered if an eagle would grab his ear with its talons, or if it would go for a larger body part, like an elbow, maybe. Thinking about it, he covered his ears with his hands.

"I need a hat," he whispered.

"Sam's been a little concerned," his sister explained to Mrs. Stein, "because he doesn't have a warm hat to wear to Alaska. So he was thinking of asking Santa Claus for one."

Mrs. Stein clapped her hands. "Sam," she said, "you are one lucky boy. Look here." She opened the door of the hall closet and pointed to a dark green plastic bag. "I was about to send all of these things to the Salvation Army." She opened the yellow plastic strip that was loosely tied at the top of the bag.

"Nightgown?" she laughed. "Guess you

don't need that. It's ripped, anyway." Mrs. Stein pulled out a blue flannel nightgown and set it aside.

"Ladies' sneakers? I thought I was going to take an aerobics class at the Y, but I never got around to it. Look — hardly worn at all." She held up some white tennis shoes. "Nope, wrong size for you, Sam. Anyway, you need warm boots in Alaska in winter. Got warm boots?"

Sam looked down at his feet. He was wearing his Velcro-closing blue sneakers with little blinking lights on the heels. "No," he muttered. "No warm boots."

Maybe the little blinking lights would scare creatures and wildlife, he thought.

"Here!" Mrs. Stein held up a dead animal triumphantly. Anastasia backed up with a look of apprehension. Sam stared.

"What is it?" he asked.

"Mink." Mrs. Stein leaned over and placed it on Sam's head. She wedged it down firmly around his ears. It felt heavy and hot, and he could feel that inside the hat one of his ears was folded and his hair was mashed.

"Great, Sam," Anastasia said. "Perfect hat for Alaska."

"I'm going to give you one other thing," Mrs. Stein said. "A going-away gift. Here you are." She took a pair of sunglasses from the drawer of the tall chest near the hall closet. "I've heard that you must really be careful in Alaska to protect your eyes. The sun can cause snow blindness."

"Mr. Fosburgh said it was night all the time," Sam pointed out.

"That's only in winter. In summer it's day all the time. So you save these sunglasses for next summer. I don't want to hear that you're having trouble with snow blindness."

Mrs. Stein tucked the glasses into his pocket, next to the flashlight and on top of the fangs.

Sam felt very uncomfortable. His pocket was crowded and bulging. His head felt like a monster head, huge and furry. He had trouble

seeing because the hat came down so low over his forehead that there was mink fringe in front of his eyes. His folded ear hurt a little. He had to go to the bathroom.

And even though he had eaten a hot dog, half an apple, some cookies, milk, and a chicken leg already this afternoon, Sam realized suddenly that he had a special kind of hungry feeling. It wasn't a not-enough-food kind of hungry. It was just a feeling that more than anything, he wanted some of his mother's lasagna.

8

Anastasia and Mrs. Stein didn't seem to notice how miserable Sam felt. They continued talking cheerfully to each other, paying no attention to the fact that right there, right in the hall beside them, stood a person who before his fifth birthday would probably be blinded by snow, chewed by bears, grabbed by talons, lost because he didn't know how to read a map, and sick because he didn't like blubber. And on top of everything else, his fangs — his precious fangs, which were the cause of everything — might get cavities, and Sam was absolutely certain there would be no dentist in Sleetmute.

Mrs. Stein's clock chimed loudly. Sam counted five chimes.

"I love that clock," Anastasia said.

"Me too," Sam said. He tilted his head back so that he could see under the fur of the hat. He looked up toward the clock.

The tall clock stood on the landing of the stairs. It had moons and stars on its face, and you could hear a slow, steady tick.

"I wind that clock once a month," Mrs. Stein said. "I open its front door and the key is inside, on a special shelf. Then I open the glass part, over the face, and put the key into the special winding slot. See up there?" She pointed.

Sam looked carefully at the clock's face and saw the narrow winding slot.

"You know what, Sam? You're old enough now to be very careful. Next time — the first of November will be the next time — you could stand on a chair, and I could show you how, and *you* could wind the clock for me! I could make you my official clock-winder. It's a little hard for me because of my arthritis. But you have young hands, Sam. You could—"

She stopped suddenly. Sam stared at Mrs. Stein and then he stared at her wonderful clock. More than anything in the world Sam wanted to be the official clock-winder.

"Sorry, Sam. I forgot," Mrs. Stein said. "You won't be here for the November clock-winding."

Sam didn't say anything at first. Then, remembering, he said, "November is Kelly Sheehan's first birthday, and Mrs. Sheehan is having a party."

"Oh, good," Mrs. Stein said. "Ice cream and cake."

"And of course November is Thanksgiving," Anastasia added.

Thanksgiving. That meant Pilgrims and Indians and the *Mayflower*. And Squanto, too. Sam loved Squanto. He wished that his own name were Squanto Krupnik.

This was Sam's second year at nursery school, and he remembered last year's Thanksgiving. In November Mrs. Bennett would be reading stories about Squanto, and holding up the book to show the pictures. The children would make crayon drawings of turkeys. They would have a feast and invite the mothers.

For last year's feast, the nursery school girls wore Pilgrim ladies' hats, and the boys wore Pilgrim men's hats, which they had made out of cardboard. The men's hats were better than the women's because the men's hats had gold buckles. Some of the Pilgrim men had cardboard hatchets, too, although the boys who had hatchets always had to take a lot of timeouts because they couldn't seem to stop hatcheting each other. Maybe this year they wouldn't have hatchets at school.

Last year, lots of mothers came, and they all brought food for the feast. Adam's mom brought celery. Leah's mom brought rolls and butter. Sam's mom had brought corn and lima beans mixed together, because that was one of the things that the Indians had taught the Pilgrims to eat.

Everybody in the whole Krupnik family hated lima beans, but Sam and his mom were good sports about it at the nursery school feast because Squanto was such a cool guy. Anyway, if you were careful when you took your helping, you could get mostly corn in the spoon. When nobody was looking, you could put the lima beans into your pocket. Later, if you had a dog, you could feed the lima beans to your dog, if your dog would eat them. Some dogs wouldn't.

Thanksgiving was a happy kind of holiday, Sam knew. But thinking about Thanksgiving suddenly made him feel sad. He felt like a Pilgrim who hadn't been invited to the feast.

While Anastasia and Mrs. Stein continued to talk, Sam wandered to a nearby window and looked across the lawn toward his own house. He could see his father's car in the driveway. He could see a light on in the kitchen window.

As he watched, his mother walked past the

window, carrying something. It looked as if she were carrying a pan of lasagna from the refrigerator side of the kitchen over to the stove side of the kitchen.

Now she had disappeared from view, but in his mind Sam could see her still, leaning over to put the pan into the oven, then standing and turning the dials to the correct temperature.

Next he pictured her walking into the dining room and opening the chest of drawers where she kept placemats. Maybe she would choose the blue and white checkered ones, Sam thought. She would count the correct number. Sam looked down at his own fingers and began to count.

One placemat for his mother. One for his father. One for his sister. One for Mrs. Stein. One for Mr. Fosburgh. One for Mrs. Sheehan. One for Kelly.

That was seven. A whole hand plus two fingers.

But there were eight blue and white checkered placemats in the drawer.

"Mom needs one more person for dinner," Sam announced. "There are only seven people, and she needs eight because of the placemats, so I guess I could —"

But before he could finish, Anastasia interrupted him. "No, there are eight people," she said. "Mr. Watson's coming. He got to talking to Mom about lasagna when he delivered the mail, and she invited him, too."

Anastasia laughed a little. "She even promised to save some uncooked lasagna pieces for him. He's thinking he might do a lasagna sculpture of ocean waves."

In his mind, Sam pictured the eighth placemat on the table. He pictured the mailman, Mr. Watson, sitting right at Sam's place, maybe even using Sam's special plate with The Little Engine That Could running around the edge. Sam loved Mr. Watson, but it made him feel sad to think of Mr. Watson eating lasagna from Sam's special plate.

Maybe, he thought, he should stop by his

house and get his plate and take it to Alaska with him.

"Also," Anastasia went on, "the Harveys are coming over later, for dessert. Even Steve."

"I thought Steve was toast!" Sam said.

Anastasia shrugged and laughed. "I changed my mind. I decided maybe I like Steve after all. And Mom figured what the heck, might as well have the whole neighborhood. Mrs. Harvey's bringing another pie.

"Remember what I told you, Sam?" she added. "It's very mature to change your mind. Only dumb babies are really stubborn about their opinions."

"Yeah, just dumb babies," Sam agreed. But he wasn't really paying attention to his sister. He was thinking about pies.

The mention of pies had brought back Sam's hungry feeling: the feeling of being uninvited, maybe of peeking in at the party and seeing everyone else enjoying dessert when there was none for him.

He decided to eat some of his running-away-to-Alaska food. He decided that he would do it privately.

"May I go to visit the flamingos?" Sam asked Mrs. Stein politely.

She nodded, and pointed, even though of course Sam knew where it was.

Leaving his sister and Mrs. Stein still chatting about old-fashioned furniture, Sam went into the bathroom off the little hall beside the kitchen. Today there were pink towels that matched the flamingos. As he always did, Sam examined the flamingos carefully, trying to figure out how they stood like that, with one leg tucked up tight against their tummies.

Standing on one leg like a flamingo was a very, very hard thing to do, but Sam was getting better at it. He could stand that way now until he counted to five, and he was hoping to get to ten. When he could stand like a flamingo all the way to ten, he would show people. Maybe he would do it at nursery school, for show-and-tell.

Of course, Sam realized suddenly, they might not have nursery school in Sleetmute.

Sam decided not to think about that. Today, for the first time, Sam didn't even bother doing his flamingo imitation. He had more important tasks. He closed the door behind him, knelt on the floor, and unzipped his traveling bag.

First he removed the heavy atlas that was on the top. Then he looked around, shoving things aside, until he found what he was looking for. *There.* The jar of peanut butter — a brand-new one with Mr. Peanut on the label — was in the corner of his bag, on top of some mashed cookies. Sam removed it. He wished that he had bread. He wished that he had a knife, or even a spoon.

But he decided that he would just plunge his finger in, scoop out a mound of peanut butter (he hoped it was super-chunk), and eat it right from his own finger. Then he could return the jar to his bag, return the atlas to his bag, zip the bag, go to the bathroom, wash his hands, dry them on one of the flamingo-pink towels, and stand briefly on one leg for the last time. Then he would insert his fangs, say goodbye, and head for Alaska before it got any darker outside.

It was a good plan. But it didn't work. Sam couldn't get the jar of Mr. Peanut open.

He twisted and twisted, but it didn't budge.

Kneeling there, staring in frustration at the unopened jar that was (he could see, looking through its glass side) filled to the top with gooey, delicious peanut butter waiting to be eaten, Sam tried to remember what his mother did when she couldn't open a jar.

Sometimes she called his father for help. Sam couldn't do that.

Sometimes she wrapped dish towel around the lid and tried again. Sam adjusted his mink hat, pushing it up away from his eyes so that he could see better. Then he wrapped a flamingo-pink towel around the jar; but the towel was too bulky, and completely unsuccessful. The jar was still closed.

Sometimes, Sam remembered, his mother tapped the lid with a knife. But Sam was not allowed to use knives. And there was no knife in Gertrude Stein's bathroom, anyway.

He did have the little flashlight in his pocket, though. Maybe that would work.

Sam tapped the lid of the Mr. Peanut jar with the small flashlight. But the lid was still tightly stuck. He tapped one more time, as hard as he could, but still the lid would not move.

Sam examined the flashlight and tested its switch, trying to illuminate one flamingo on the wallpaper. But the little flashlight hadn't survived being banged on the jar. It didn't work anymore.

Sam sighed. He put the broken flashlight on the floor.

Sometimes, Sam remembered, his mom ran hot water over a stuck lid. That was a possibility. Carefully he turned on the faucet that said H — H was for Hot, Sam knew — and held the jar of peanut butter under the running water.

Then, carefully, he turned the water off, dried the jar with a flamingo-pink towel, and tried again to twist off the lid. It didn't budge.

There was only one last thing to try. Sam remembered that sometimes, when a lid was stuck, his mother rapped it hard against the countertop in the kitchen. He had watched her do it many times.

Mrs. Stein's bathroom had no counters. But the floor was tile in little white diamond shapes. It was good and hard. Carefully Sam knelt on the rug, held the Mr. Peanut jar, and bashed it against the tile floor.

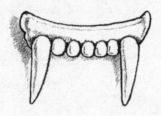

9

Sam? Are you okay? What's going on in there? Why are you crying?" Anastasia was knocking on the door and calling to him.

The door opened and he looked up at his sister from the rug where he was sitting.

"I'm having a bad time," Sam wailed.

Anastasia stared at him for a minute. Squinting through the mink fur, Sam could see Gertrude Stein, too, standing beside Anastasia and peering into the bathroom.

"I can see that, Sam," Anastasia said at last. She came into the bathroom and knelt beside him on the rug.

Her voice was sympathetic. "You've got a whole mess of problems here, Sam," she said. "First of all, the hat. The hat has to go so you can see. Do you mind if I remove your hat?"

Sam shook his head.

Anastasia lifted off the mink hat and handed it to Gertrude Stein.

"There," Anastasia said. "That hat is toast."

Sam giggled a little. His head felt much better without the hat, and he liked it when Anastasia said something was toast.

"Gonzo," Sam said. *"Kaput."*

Anastasia smoothed his hair, which had been folded and flattened and was a little sweaty, too.

"Next," she said, "you have a pretty bad case of Hat Hair. We can fix that, though." She reached over for a hairbrush that was on a shelf. "Mind if I use this, Mrs. Stein?" she asked.

Gertrude Stein said, "Please. Be my guest."

So Anastasia brushed Sam's hair gently. She held her hand cupped around his chin while she did it, just the way his mother always did. It felt nice.

"Next," Anastasia said, "about your eyebrows and the mustache."

Sam had forgotten about his eyebrows and mustache. "What about them?" he asked. "Are they toast?"

"They're about to be," Anastasia said. She ran some warm water over a washcloth and washed his face gently, still cupping his chin in one hand. That felt nice, too.

The Band-Aid on his forehead slid off and she put it into the wastebasket.

"Next," Anastasia said, "your finger is bleeding a little. Did you know that?"

Sam didn't. He looked down. The pointer finger on his right hand was bleeding just a little.

"Stand up, Sam." His sister helped him to his feet. She removed the wrinkled Band-Aid from the back of his hand and deposited it into the wastebasket with the first one. Then she held his hand under the faucet and ran some cold water over his injured finger. Then she dried it gently with a flamingo-pink towel. The bleeding had stopped.

"Band-Aids in the medicine cabinet," Gertrude Stein directed. "No stars or hearts, though."

Anastasia found a small pinkish-beige Band-Aid, unwrapped it, and bandaged Sam's wounded finger carefully.

"Next?" she asked.

Sam sighed. "The flashlight broke," he told her, and pointed to the little flashlight, which had rolled into a corner of the bathroom floor.

Anastasia retrieved Mr. Fosburgh's flashlight. She tried the switch, shook the flashlight, and tried again. Then she dropped it into the wastebasket.

"Toast?" Sam asked.

Anastasia nodded. "Toast. We'll get him a new one."

"Next?" she said.

Sam thought. There seemed to be a lot of nexts. "The cookies," he admitted. "Mrs. Stein's cookies. They're toast." He pointed to the bag, and Anastasia looked inside.

"They're not toast," Anastasia said. "They're crumbs. We'll dump them out."

"I have lots of cookies, Sam," Mrs. Stein added. "I was going to take a batch over to your mother's this evening. No problem."

"The orange looks okay," Anastasia said, removing it from the bag. She turned it around in her hands.

"And your bear's cool," she said, removing Sam's bear and holding it up. "Just a little crumby." She brushed some cookie crumbs from the bear and handed him to Sam.

Sam hugged his bear and smelled the familiar smell of fake fur that made him think of toothpaste, bedtime, stories, and goodnight kisses.

"Mittens are okay. Blanket's okay. Towel's okay, I think, but it smells horrible." Anastasia sniffed the rolled-up towel and made a face. "Yuck. That's Dad's gym towel, Sam. It was waiting to be washed." She set it aside.

"Atlas? Let me look." She lifted the heavy book and examined it carefully. "Good. It's fine, Sam. No damage. Just a few crumbs.

"You feeling better?" she asked Sam.

Sam nodded. He was feeling much, much better.

"Okay, then. Any more problems I can help you deal with?"

Sam sighed. There were two more problems, both of them serious, and he would not be able to hide either of them forever. He stepped aside and pointed to the floor behind him. He had draped a flamingo-pink towel over the disaster. He watched as Anastasia lifted the towel.

"I *thought* I heard something smash," Anastasia said. "Is this how you cut your finger?"

Sam nodded. He was embarrassed.

"Mrs. Stein," Anastasia said, "we need a dustpan, I think. And, let's see, maybe a scrub brush and some hot water."

"Coming up," Gertrude Stein said, and she

opened the broom closet door between the bathroom and the kitchen.

Ten minutes later, the bathroom floor was clean and gleaming. Anastasia picked up the crumpled towels, the bucket of hot water, and the wastebasket containing the remains of the flashlight and the peanut butter jar.

"You're amazing, Sam," she said, looking around. "Not many people could create that much chaos in that short a time."

Sam thought about that. It *did* seem amazing. Of course his mother had always called him her super-spectacular son. Maybe she was right.

Maybe he liked his mother again, Sam realized.

"Is that it?" his sister asked. "Everything fixed now?"

Sam didn't say anything. His sister had not noticed the other serious problem, and he decided not to tell her just yet.

Anastasia left the bathroom. Sam began to follow her, then turned back.

Alone in the newly cleaned, sweet-smelling bathroom, Sam looked at the wallpaper with its amazing pink flamingos. There they stood, each on one skinny leg, their long necks stretched high or curled into upside-down question marks, their heads in impossible places, their eyes calm. They looked as if their lives were turning out just right.

Sam sighed. Then, very carefully, holding his breath, Sam stood on one leg. He raised his other leg slowly, folding it at the knee like a flamingo. He steadied himself, folded his arms like wings, stretched his neck, then began to count.

This time he got to seven, but it was very uncomfortable standing like a flamingo.

"There goes Dad, over to get Mr. Fosburgh." Anastasia watched from Mrs. Stein's front window as Mr. Krupnik headed across the street. Sam watched with her. In a minute, Sam knew, his daddy would push Mr. Fosburgh's wheelchair down the ramp beside his porch steps. He would wheel Mr.

Fosburgh across the street to their own back steps, turn the wheelchair around, and bumpety-bump it up very carefully. "Hold on to your hat," Sam's dad would say to Mr. Fosburgh. He always said that, even though Mr. Fosburgh never ever wore a hat.

Mrs. Stein was putting on her coat. She had a bag of chocolate chip cookies on the hall table, ready to take to the Krupniks' house.

"Sam?" Anastasia said. "Here's the deal. You can start off now to Alaska, but it's getting dark out, and your flashlight is broken, and it's kind of cold now, and you don't have a hat . . ."

Sam had his hand in his pocket. He felt his fangs. He looked at the floor. He was thinking about his other serious problem, which was a secret.

"And probably," Anastasia went on, "Mrs. Stein would give you a few more cookies—"

"Yes," Gertrude Stein said. "I certainly would."

"But frankly, Sam," Anastasia continued, "cookies are not a great diet for a cold climate.

Mom would be thrilled if you'd come back to the house and have some lasagna."

"Would she let me —" Sam began.

"No," Anastasia said. "Mom will not let you wear fangs."

Sam sighed. "So I have to go live with walruses," he said, and he knew, even as he was saying it, that he was using a whiny voice.

"*Walruses?*" Anastasia repeated. "Why walruses?"

"Because of fangs," Sam explained.

Anastasia looked at him. "Sam," she said, "walruses don't have fangs."

He looked up, still feeling the grit-covered plastic in his pocket. "Yes, they do. Walruses lie around in a pile and they have fangs sticking right out by their whiskers. I saw them in a video at nursery school."

"*Sam,*" his sister said, "those aren't fangs. Those are *tusks!*"

Tusks. The minute he heard Anastasia say it, he knew she was right. He had simply forgotten.

"Creatures with tusks don't even *like* creatures with fangs," Mrs. Stein said. "I'm fairly certain of that. I think you might even be in danger, Sam, if you go to Alaska."

Anastasia looked back through the window. "There's Mrs. Harvey, carrying a pie, heading for our house. I wonder what kind of pie she made."

I hope cherry, Sam found himself thinking. Inside his pocket, he held his fangs very tightly.

"And look!" Anastasia added. "There's Lowell Watson, without his mailbag! I don't think I've ever seen him without his mailbag. What's he carrying?"

Sam moved toward the window and peered out. He looked very carefully as Mr. Watson passed under the street light, which had just come on. The mailman was carrying something very carefully in front of him with both hands, and he was headed to the Krupniks' house.

"He made me a rigatoni igloo!" Sam said in awe.

"A *what?*" Anastasia and Mrs. Stein said at the same time. Sam didn't bother to explain. He just watched happily as his friend, Lowell Watson, carried the rounded pasta igloo — Sam could see that it even had a little chimney — up the steps to the Krupniks' front door.

Watching, Sam wiggled in excitement, and was suddenly reminded of his secret, serious, and somewhat uncomfortable problem.

"I wet my pants," he announced. "And I'm going home."

"Sam?" Anastasia said. "What about —"

"My fangs?" With his hand deep in his pocket, Sam squeezed his fangs very hard with his hand and could feel them crack. He squeezed harder and felt them break in half.

"I changed my mind," Sam said. "It's a very grown-up thing to do. And anyway," he added, "these fangs are toast."

10

Fresh from the bathtub, Sam stood in his bedroom wrapped in a towel while his sister found clean clothes for him. He could smell the wonderful smell of lasagna coming from the kitchen below. He could hear the voices of all the neighbors, even the excited squeals of Kelly Sheehan, who was playing with some of Sam's blocks on the living room rug. The Sheehans had just arrived, and Sam wondered if maybe, because it was sort of a party, they had dressed Kelly in party clothes: maybe a little sailor suit, or perhaps a frilly dress, depending on whether Kelly was a boy or a girl.

He lifted one leg and then the other, a little like a flamingo, as Anastasia guided his feet into his underpants. Then she helped him with his socks. She pulled a red turtleneck shirt down over his head, and smoothed his hair after his head popped through the hole.

"Where's a clean pair of jeans, Sam?" his sister asked, and he pointed to his closet.

When she opened the closet door, he glimpsed something familiar on the shelf inside. "My Etch A Sketch!" Sam cried.

Anastasia lifted it down from the shelf. "You want it? You never play with it," she said. "Remember how we used to fool around with it after last Christmas but it was too hard to make curvy lines, and too boring just to make straight ones?"

Sam took it from her and set it on the table beside his bed. He lifted his feet one by one and Anastasia pulled his jeans up and adjusted the waist. "I'm taking it to school tomorrow," he told her. "I'm giving it to my friend Adam."

"You're so generous, Sam," his sister said,

smoothing his hair again. "Most guys your age wouldn't give away their toys."

Sam sat on the floor and pulled his sneakers on. He didn't tell Anastasia, but he was thinking that he wasn't generous at all. He was just *dumb.* He was a dumb guy who used to have an Etch A Sketch. He sighed, and followed his sister down the stairs.

"Hey, Sam! Welcome home!" Mr. Fosburgh said as Sam trotted into the living room. "I'm so glad you changed your mind!" The wheelchair was in the corner by the end of the couch, and when Mr. Fosburgh held out his arms, Sam went and climbed onto his lap. Sam couldn't drive the wheelchair in his own house because of the rugs. Mr. Fosburgh's house had no rugs. When he was at the Krupniks' house, Sam's daddy had to push the chair carefully from one room to the next. But Sam still loved to sit on Mr. Fosburgh's lap.

"Me too, Sam," Gertrude Stein said, smiling. She was wearing a pretty flowered dress and sitting on the couch next to Mrs. Sheehan.

"Me too, Sam," said Mrs. Sheehan.

From his perch on Mr. Fosburgh's lap, Sam looked over to the side of the living room where Kelly Sheehan sat arranging the bright wooden blocks and laughing. Kelly was wearing something that looked like a yellow blanket with feet. *Rats.* Kelly was wearing pajamas, Sam realized. So he would have to wait till another time to find out what Kelly was.

"Since I'm back," Sam announced, "I can go to Kelly's birthday party!"

"That's right," Mrs. Sheehan said. "You can help frost the cake, too, Sam."

"And you'll be here for Thanksgiving, too, Sam! And Halloween before that," his mother pointed out. "I'm so glad you decided to return."

Mr. Watson, the mailman, came in from the kitchen, where he'd been talking to Sam's daddy and helping to put the finishing touches on the dinner. "Did I hear the word Halloween?"

Sam nodded eagerly. He had forgotten about Halloween. He had come very close to

missing Halloween by going to Alaska to lie around in a pile with walruses.

"It's coming up pretty soon, Sam," Mr. Watson said. "Know how I know? Because I've started seeing orange envelopes in the mail. People are starting to send Halloween cards.

"Happy Halloween in advance, Sam," Mr. Watson said. "I'm glad you changed your mind about Alaska."

Then Mr. Watson closed his eyes, frowned, and said quietly, "Eek."

Sam looked nervously around to see whether a mouse had run across the room. But there was nothing there, and no one else had noticed.

"Mrs. Bennett sent a notice, Sam," his mother told him. "Halloween party next Friday at school. We'll have to start making a costume. I was thinking about maybe a bunny. I figured I could cover some cardboard with fake fur for ears."

Sam stared at his mother. A *bunny*? He didn't want to hurt his mom's feelings, because he liked her again and she had made lasagna for dinner, but a *bunny*?

"Katherine," Gertrude Stein suggested, "maybe you could do a bunny costume for Kelly. Kelly would be a cute bunny. And then maybe Sam could be, oh, something ferocious, like a *wolf*."

Sam grinned at Mrs. Stein. That was a great idea: something ferocious. He formed his fingers into claws and tried a toothy wolfish snarl.

"Oh," his mother said. "Something ferocious. I see what you mean. Sure, Sam. I could do a wolf costume, I think."

"Announcement!" Sam's father entered the living room, holding a glass. He tapped on the glass with a spoon to get everyone's attention.

Everyone looked up except Kelly, who continued banging blocks together.

"Dinner's on the table," Mr. Krupnik said. "I brought Sam's old high chair down from the attic for Kelly. And I put two leaves in the table so there's room for all of us, even though the chairs don't match.

"And the centerpiece is compliments of our talented mailman, Lowell Watson."

Mr. Watson bowed proudly. "It's my first work in rigatoni," he confessed.

"It's certainly the first rigatoni igloo I've ever seen," Mr. Krupnik said.

"It's in honor of Sam," Mr. Watson explained, "even though I'm very glad he decided to stay here after all. Probably someday Sam will visit Alaska."

"Yes, probably someday," Sam said.

"Eek," Mr. Watson said suddenly, in a low, puzzled voice. No one seemed to hear him, but Sam looked around, wondering briefly again if the mailman had seen a mouse, or some other kind of creature. There were never any mice in the Krupniks' house, although once Anastasia's gerbils had gotten out of their cage. But Sam didn't see anything scurrying past in the corners, the way they had occasionally seen the gerbils until they were captured.

"And," Sam's dad went on, ignoring — or maybe not hearing — Lowell Watson's "eek"

— "there's a little gift in front of each plate. You can open them after dessert."

Sam climbed down from Mr. Fosburgh's lap and ran eagerly into the dining room. Sure enough, a small wrapped package was at each place. And it wasn't even anyone's birthday, or Christmas.

Someone lifted Kelly into the highchair, and while Kelly banged a spoon loudly on the tray, Mrs. Krupnik served lasagna and they passed a big bowl of salad around. Sam heaped his Little Engine That Could plate with food and felt very glad that he had been so mature and had changed his mind.

He wondered, though, about two things. He wondered what the little presents were. Also, watching the mailman's lips move once again, Sam wondered nervously why Mr. Watson was murmuring "Eek" so often.

"That must be the Harveys at the back door," Mrs. Krupnik said as she was clearing the plates. "She brought over a pie earlier —"

"Cherry?" asked Sam, hoping that it was.

"No, I think it's apple. But it looks yummy, Sam. Anyway, then she went back to serve their dinner, and here they are for dessert, with Mr. Harvey and Steve. Anastasia, if you go let them in, I'll start slicing pies."

Sam's father brought more chairs from the kitchen — and three more little wrapped gifts for the newest guests — and the Harveys joined the group around the table.

Tasting the warm cinnamon-flavored apple pie, with a small slice of banana cream waiting, Sam looked happily around the table at all of his friends and family. How could he have thought about running away to lie in a pile of walruses, when right here, right in his own neighborhood, were so many people who needed him so much?

Mr. Fosburgh, unless he went soon to a hypnotist, would probably set fire to his house once again, and Sam would have to go out to supervise the hook-and-ladder truck as it rescued him one more time.

Gertrude Stein, with the cat-racks on her eyes, would still depend on Sam to tell her what color things were, to help consume the cookies that she baked each day, and to wind her tall clock with its special key.

"Since I didn't go to Alaska, please can I wind your clock in November?" he asked Mrs. Stein eagerly.

"Why, of course," Mrs. Stein replied. "And December and January, too, Sam."

"And please can I help Kelly blow out the birthday cake candle?" he asked Mrs. Sheehan.

"We're counting on it," Mrs. Sheehan told him.

Sam looked at Mr. Watson, trying to figure out ways in which he could help the mailman, now that he wouldn't be going to Alaska. But Mr. Watson, who had finished his pie, was sitting quietly at his place, with his eyes closed. "Eek," he was saying. "*Eek.*"

One by one, except for Kelly, who was busy smearing banana cream pie all over the highchair tray, everyone stopped talking, put down their forks, and stared at Mr. Watson.

Finally Mrs. Krupnik said gently, "Lowell? Is something wrong?"

Lowell Watson opened his eyes, grinned broadly, and said in a loud, satisfied voice, "Nine nine five seven eight!"

"Excuse me?" Mrs. Krupnik replied, with a worried look.

"It was driving me crazy that I couldn't think of it," Mr. Watson said. "It's the ZIP code for Eek."

"*Eek?*" several people said at once.

"It's a town in Alaska," Mr. Watson explained. "I'm not exactly sure of the location."

"Well," Mr. Fosburgh said, "luckily, we happen to have a terrific atlas right here. Sam, is it still in your traveling bag?"

Sam nodded.

"Shall we find Eek for Mr. Watson?"

Sam frowned. He didn't really care that much about Alaska anymore. "Maybe later," he said. "Right now, let's open our presents."

11

Mrs. Krupnik smiled. "Well," she said, "this afternoon, after I invited you all over, I thought it might be fun to have little door prizes. So I called Sam's dad at his office and asked if he'd mind running an errand—"

Myron Krupnik grinned. "I was in the middle of a very boring meeting," he said. "So I was happy to have an excuse to go shopping."

"I could have done it myself, of course, but I was hoping that at any minute Sam might decide to come home."

"I didn't," Sam said. "I just kept traveling all afternoon. I traveled around in a big circle.

And now I can see you all around!" he said. "And you can see me around, too!"

"See you around, Sam," Mr. Watson replied cheerfully.

Kelly Sheehan looked up, laughed, and banged one small fist on the highchair tray.

"Does Kelly know about circles?" Sam asked with interest.

"I don't think so," Kelly's mom replied. "Not yet."

"You have to learn shapes before you start nursery school," Sam told her. "You have to know shapes and how to go to the bathroom."

"Oh, dear," Kelly's mom said. "Maybe you could help us work on both of those things with Kelly."

"I will," Sam promised. There was going to be a lot for him to do in the neighborhood, now that he wasn't going to Alaska. He hadn't realized how much everybody needed him.

Anastasia gave him a look. Sam cringed a little, but he was grateful that his sister hadn't told anybody that he had wet his pants that afternoon. It was tough, when you were traveling, to attend to everything.

"Earth to Sam," his mother said.

"Sorry," Sam said, and started listening again.

"Anyway," Mrs. Krupnik went on, "Sam's dad did the buying, after I gave him instructions. And I wrapped everything. Some of you got identical gifts. Let's see — Steve? You and your father have the same. Why don't you open yours?"

So Mr. Harvey and Steve opened their gifts while everyone watched. Then while everyone still watched, they put on their glasses with fake noses attached and posed. Sam giggled. Steve Harvey's father was a sportscaster for the local TV channel, and they'd all seen him looking very handsome on television while he described the Celtics games. Now he looked like a clown.

So did Steve. He stuck his tongue out and crossed his eyes.

"Next?" Mrs. Krupnik said. "Let's see. Lowell. Why don't you try yours?"

So Lowell Watson opened his little package, took out his fake mustache, and pasted it carefully to his upper lip. It was a blond mustache, which looked a little odd on Mr. Watson, who was African American; but he wore it with dignity and looked quite sophisticated. "I think I might try wearing it to choir practice at my church," he announced. "Thank you, Katherine."

"Myron, you know what yours is, because you bought it. But open it anyway. And Mr. Fosburgh, yours is just the same as Myron's." Sam watched as Mr. Fosburgh and his father both unwrapped plastic cigars. They inserted them into their mouths and puffed dramatically.

"Maybe, Myron, you could puff on that instead of your pipe?" Mrs. Krupnik suggested. She really hated her husband's pipe. "And Mr. Fosburgh . . ."

Mr. Krupnik and Mr. Fosburgh both looked guilty and miserable. They continued chewing on their plastic cigars.

"It's very grown-up to change your mind about things," Sam told them.

Mr. Fosburgh sighed. "I know," he said. "I'm going to the hypnotist soon."

Myron Krupnik sighed. "I'll go with you," he said with a mournful look.

Sam hoped his would be next. He wondered if he would get a cigar, but hoped not. He really, really wanted a fake nose. He could see that the glasses hooked around your ears like real glasses, and the nose fit right over your real nose. Sam could imagine the amazed looks at nursery school when he arrived wearing a big pink fake nose.

But his mother turned to the women: Mrs. Stein, Mrs. Sheehan, and Mrs. Harvey. She smiled at them apologetically.

"I'm afraid I ran out of ideas for the women," she explained. "So ours are all the same. Mine, too, and Anastasia's." Sam's mom began to unwrap her package. So did his sister, and the women guests.

They each took out bright red wax lips. Gertrude Stein inserted hers into her mouth and looked around the room with a very haughty look. Sam started to laugh.

Anastasia tried to put her lips on but she was laughing too hard. Finally, after a couple of tries, she had the lips in the right place, and she posed with Steve, in his glasses and nose, who was sitting beside her.

Sam stared at his mother, who actually looked a little scary to him with the big bright lips. He heard a wail, and realized that Kelly, too, was wide-eyed, frightened, and beginning to cry. Mrs. Sheehan quickly took her lips off and smiled at her baby.

Kelly stopped crying and reached for the red lips.

"Those are just for the ladies, Kelly," Sam said.

"It's okay," Mrs. Sheehan told him. She handed Kelly her wax lips. "Kelly's a little lady, after all."

"Oh," said Sam. "*Oh!*" Funny, he thought, how finally you figured stuff out if you paid attention.

"Yuzheonnny—" Anastasia began to say. She took her lips off and tried again. "You're the only one left, Sam," Anastasia said. "What's yours?"

"Go ahead, Sam," his mother told him.

So Sam picked up his present. He felt it through the wrapping. It felt very familiar. It felt familiar because he'd been feeling something exactly like it all afternoon, in his pocket.

Slowly he unwrapped the plastic fangs. He held them in his hand and looked at them a long time. Then he looked at his mom.

She was smiling at him. "Will you forgive me, Sam?" she asked. "I've changed my mind."

"It's a very grown-up thing to change your mind," Sam said once again. He turned the fangs around in his hand and thought that it would be polite, since they were a gift, to insert them into his mouth.

"But I changed my mind, too," he said to his mother at last. "Would it be okay if I trade them for a nose?"

Turn the page
for a sneak peek
at the next book
in the series,

Zooman Sam!

→

1

"What are you doing, Sam?" his mother called from the bottom of the stairs. "Dinner will be ready soon!"

"Nothing," Sam called back from his bedroom. *Nothing* wasn't exactly true. But it was what you said when it was too hard to describe the truth. The truth would have been "I'm looking at my clothes."

But then his mom would have said, "Why are you looking at your clothes? Is there something wrong with your clothes?" and she would have come up the stairs, and then Sam would have tried to explain *why* he was looking at all his clothes, and his mom would have noticed that he'd made a mess in his closet because when he stood on a chair and pushed the hangers to one side, they all fell down, and now everything was in a heap, and Sam *planned* to pick them all up and hang them again and he just hadn't done it yet, but his mom wouldn't understand that, and she'd probably get mad, and—

It was easier to say "Nothing."

"We're having chicken," his mom called, and he could hear her feet going back to the kitchen. Then he could hear the thumping of dog feet. Sam laughed a little. He knew it was Sleuth, the Krupniks' dog. Like most dogs, Sleuth understood "Come," and "Sit," though he didn't always choose to obey. But unlike most dogs, somehow Sleuth could recognize any word that related to food. And Sam's mom had said "chicken," so Sleuth, who spent most of his time sleeping (and probably dreaming of food), had leaped up to follow Mrs. Krupnik down the hall.

Sam didn't even care about chicken. He was too absorbed in his search. He began to poke through the pile of clothes on the floor of the closet.

He picked up a blue and white sailor suit and made a face. He remembered the wedding at which he had worn it. His sister, Anastasia, had been a bridesmaid, and she wore a beautiful dress. She looked like a princess, or like a Barbie. Sam wouldn't have minded if he could have dressed like a prince, or a Ken. He would have worn a tuxedo. Sam thought tuxedos were cool.

But instead, his mom had made him wear that dumb sailor suit. It had short pants. His mom told him that it made him look like Popeye, and she had even drawn a marking-pen anchor tattoo on his arm, under the sleeve. But it wasn't true, about Popeye. The suit was just a dumb baby sailor suit, and everybody at the wedding said he looked cute. Sam didn't want to look cute. He wanted to look tough and mean. He decided he would never, ever wear the sailor suit again. He rolled it into a ball and threw it into the darkest corner of the closet, next to the folded-up stroller.

Sam noticed his Osh-Kosh overalls hanging from a hook. He stood on the chair and took them down. He liked his overalls. His sister had some just like them, and sometimes he and Anastasia wore their overalls on the same day. Their dad called them Ma and Pa Kettle when they wore their overalls.

Sam liked that. He didn't know who Ma and Pa Kettle were, but he liked the sound of those names.

But today the overalls were not what Sam needed. He thought about climbing up to re-hang them on their hook, but that was too much bother. He rolled them up and threw them into the other corner of the closet, where they settled in a heap on top of his ant farm.

"Five minutes till dinner! Wash your hands, please!"

Hearing his mother's voice, Sam sighed.

He looked at the clothes remaining in the pile that had fallen from the rod. Halfheartedly he picked up his bright yellow raincoat and thought about it for a minute. He liked his raincoat. But today it was not what he needed. He dropped the raincoat on the floor on top of his red snowsuit.

He looked toward the other side of the room, where he had already dumped the clothes he had taken from his bureau drawers. Socks and underpants and T-shirts and sweaters and jeans were strewn across the rug. His Superman pajamas dangled across the arm of the rocking chair, and a sweatshirt that said HARVARD UNIVERSITY had somehow landed on the head of Sam's old rocking horse.

None of the clothes were right. Sam felt like a failure. He felt like the biggest, dumbest poop-head in the world. He began to cry. He kicked the side of his bed in frustration, and his cat, who had been sleeping in her usual place beside Sam's teddy bear, woke in surprise. She jumped from the bed with an irritated swish of her tail, gave Sam a disgusted look, and left the room.

That was the final blow. Even his cat hated him. Sam began to cry harder.

"Everybody! Dinner's on the table! Come right now!"